faith matters

God is reaching out
to you
He says to just hold on
His guidance is never wrong

what He tears down
He rebuilds better
when you suffer through it
together
whatever
is in His word
will manifest
as He tests
the new foundation
He gives a glimpse
of each creation

the transformation
into faith
the building blocks
of hope

you can go
wherever
His word says

Here's to the losers
Substance abusers
To the rejects
All the imperfects
To the retarded
And the broken-hearted
To the starving masses
And the lower classes

'Cause I think we're beautiful

- Kory Clarke

the unseen world

poetry in the light volume 3 of Frank DeF

Special thanks to:
Kairos Outside for allowing me to donate
books to their organization.

Special thanks to:
Orestes Rodriguez for translating
7 Prayers into Spanish

De Tonti of the Iron Hand

And the Exploration of the Mississippi

De Tonti of the Iron Hand

And the Exploration of the Mississippi

By
Ann Heagney

Illustrated by Rus Anderson

HILLSIDE EDUCATION

Cover and interior book design by Mary Jo Loboda

Cover Image: *La Salle's Party Entering the Mississippi in Canoes, 1682* by
George Catlin, National Gallery of Art, Used by permission

ISBN: 978-0-9976647-4-4

Hillside Education
475 Bidwell Hill Road
Lake Ariel, PA 18436
www.hillsideeducation.com

Contents

Chapter 1

ENTER CAPTAIN IRON HAND

The colors were going up over Fort St. Joseph on the south shore of Lake Michigan one morning late in October, 1681. Outside the stockade a strange, almost outlandish young figure was standing at salute. The patriotic gesture seemed to indicate that the boy was French, yet he looked like one of the Abenakis or Mohegans who were camped around the fortress.

His head was shaved like that of a savage; nothing was left but a lock on the crown and a fringe around the temples. The effect was fantastic, for his hair was medium brown and his blue-gray eyes looked startlingly pale in a face bronzed by wind and weather. He was dressed in wild animal skins and was strong and agile as any red man.

A grizzled head poked out of the fort window and a grinning face looked down over the stockade. "Good day, White Moose," the soldier called with a teasing laugh.

"My name is Gabriel La Grue, Sergeant Ako," said the boy in very good French.

Another middle-aged man came out of the fort. He walked with a limp and his face, though round and jovial, was seamed by the rugged marks of a frontiersman's life.

"When are you going to stop teasing young Gabriel, Sergeant?" he asked. "You know he's as white as we are even if he does look and act like a savage. And where could you find so loyal a Frenchman, saluting the flag as he does every morning?"

It was true, for young Gabriel La Grue thrilled every time he saw the banner with the golden fleur-de-lis of His Majesty Louis XIV floating out over the fort, over the mingled waters of St. Joseph River and Lake Michigan.

The fort stood on a high plateau that nature had formed in the shape of a triangle. Two sides were protected by water, the third fell away to a deep ravine. The fort itself was not large, forty feet long by thirty wide, with a separate magazine or storeroom for gunpowder and other explosives. Two years before the explorer René Robert Cavelier, better known as the Sieur de La Salle, had built it to protect his men and supplies from the fierce warlike Iroquois and their allies. Besides the quarters for officers and men, there was within the stockade a bark cabin that served as a chapel whenever a missionary came to the outpost.

La Salle had left a few men of his company in charge and then early the following year a roving band of Indians from faraway New England had pitched their lodges around the fort. They were allies of the French and glad to join up with La Salle. They had sworn a solemn oath to follow him as their chief.

Gabriel La Grue owed his life to these friendly Indians. Six years before, when he was only nine, they had rescued him from an Iroquois raiding party that had surprised the little French settlement to which his parents belonged. The Abenakis had driven off the hated Iroquois but not before the latter had massacred the white settlers. The small boy was the only survivor, so the friendly Indians had taken him away with them.

"I was only joking, lad," Sergeant Ako said. "I hear the Indians call you White Moose and sometimes, when you plunge naked into the lake like the rest of them, I've noticed the figure of a wolf tattooed on your thigh."

"It's the sign of the Abenakis," the boy explained gravely. "They are called the Wolves, and White Moose is the name they gave me. But I have never forgotten my real name nor the language of my own people."

"Ah, that's the spirit," the jolly man applauded. "I'm called two different ways myself. My real name is Antoine Auguel but I'm known as 'the Picard' because I come from Picardy."

Michael Ako then gave the boy a curious glance. "Well, Gabriel La Grue, you'll never wash the Indian sign away. It's there to stay. Now why did you let them put their mark on you if you're so set on being white?"

The boy threw back his head in a spirited gesture. "I'm proud to bear the sign. When an Indian boy becomes fourteen he is put through tests to prove his courage and endurance and will power. He must never show fear or shrink from pain or faint from weakness. If he passes the test, he is given his tribal name and mark—"

"And you showed the savages that a white boy is as tough as the best of them," Ako broke in with an approving nod.

Such praise from the veteran brought a flush of pleasure to Gabriel's tanned cheeks. "Old Medicine Snake— he's the Mohegan wizard—hoped I would show the white feather," he recalled, laughing a bit over the memory.

He could still see the sly mocking smile on the tricky red man's face and the narrow cunning eyes sneering at him as the sharp thorns pricked the holes through his skin until the blood flowed. Then a little water mixed with a powder made from the charcoal of a walnut branch burned in the fire was forced into his flesh as the tattoo was made.

"Does the medicine man hold a grudge against you because you're white?"

The boy shook his head thoughtfully. "It's our Christian religion he detests—maybe it's fear. Many of these Indians have been baptized by the missionaries and no longer believe in his magic powers. We seldom see a priest or have a chance to hear Mass but we've kept the Faith. And I still have this."

Gabriel put a hand inside his deerhide tunic and pulled out a small blue rosary. "It was my mother's."

This was the only reminder of his parents the boy had left, but there was something more: his father's old firelock gun. Gabriel had seen it in the hands of one of the Mohegan chiefs, Thunder Hawk, and knew it to be rightfully his, for his father's initials were carved on the breech. The fire stick, as the Indians called it, had made Thunder Hawk a power among his people but Gabriel held him in secret contempt. Always the theft had rankled in his mind, perhaps because he was only a boy and dared not claim what belonged to him.

The Picard was looking at him with a kindly smile. "Someday—perhaps sooner than you think, my boy—a priest will come to St. Joseph's."

This was to happen sooner than anyone expected. That same day, as the golden sunset made a spangled glory of the lake, a longboat came gliding out of the east. The slanting rays outlined the figures of six passengers, and one wore the gray robe and peaked hood of the Franciscans.

Before the twilight shadows had turned to darkness, word came to the Indian village that the friar was opening the chapel and would say Mass next morning at 6 o'clock. His name was Father Zenobius Membré and this was his first visit to Fort St. Joseph.

Gabriel was there early next day to ask if he might serve Mass. "I don't know Latin, Father," he began, "but I could move the book and pour the water and wine and ring the bell."

Father Zenobius had the kindest, clearest blue eyes Gabriel had ever seen. He looked about forty but there was something innocent, almost childlike in his manner that reached out and warmed Gabriel's heart. "I'll be happy to have you for my server," he said, smiling. He laid a friendly hand on Gabriel's shoulder. "Are you not the son of a Frenchman?"

A sudden grin lighted up the boy's tanned face. "I'm not a half-breed, Father, though I may look like one." And before he knew it, he was telling this gentle, understanding man all about himself.

As they talked, the little bark chapel was filling up with Christian Abenakis and Mohegans. Soon the men from the fort came in and behind them strode down the narrow aisle the five men who had come with Father Zenobius. Gabriel found it hard to keep from staring at the newcomers, especially at their leader.

The other four were plainly French but this man was very dark with ruddy cheeks and brilliant black eyes. His hair was as black as an Indian's but soft and curling, and he carried himself with the proud look of a military commandant. However Gabriel noticed that his right shoulder sagged down in an odd way and the arm hung heavily at his side. On his right hand he wore a black leather glove but none on the left. And that seemed unusual, too.

"What is his name?" Gabriel whispered to Father Zenobius, his eyes fixed on the strange but impressive figure.

"He is Captain Henri de Tonti," the friar answered, "sent by Chevalier de la Salle. He has come in advance to prepare the way for our great commander."

When the Mass was over Gabriel stayed to help Father Zenobius put away the altar vessels and vestments. As they did this the priest told him something about his own life—how he had dreamed of going to faraway places and preaching the Faith to strange, savage peoples when he was just a schoolboy in France; how the dream had come true when he joined the Recollects, a strict branch of the Franciscans, who were doing heroic work in the New World.

"But I am not brave at all and not much of a missionary, I'm afraid. Not if you were to judge by the number of pagans I've baptized since I came six years ago," he said in his simple, humble way.

"It's not your fault, Father," cried Gabriel warmly. "Many Indians have hard and cruel hearts, but you'll find ours different here at St. Joseph's. Will you teach me Latin, Father, so I can really serve Mass?"

Father Zenobius looked into the eager young face and answered gently: "I would gladly, my son, but we are leaving soon on a great expedition. You will hear about our plans at the meeting."

Gabriel was tingling with excitement and curiosity when the summons came to go to the fort. What was the "great expedition" being planned? What had De La Salle's men to say to the village people?

Inside the fort a long table had been placed and here in the center sat De Tonti with his flashing eyes and gloved hand.

To his right sat a youngish man with a highborn look, before him a roll of parchment and quill pen. Next to him was an older man who also had a certain air of distinction, and beside him was Father Zenobius.

To De Tonti's left—and Gabriel was surprised at this—sat the Mohegan Chief Thunder Hawk with his crony, Medicine Snake, at his side. Next was the head chief of the nation, old Sitting Bear, an Abenaki, and his son, Chief Little Wolf. The Indians squatted in a wide circle on the stone floor.

The medicine man had an impassive look on his face, but Gabriel caught him darting baneful glances toward the gray-robed figure of the French friar. He kept whispering in Thunder Hawk's ear as though giving him instructions, and the pagan chief nodded in agreement.

After a brief parley, De Tonti rose and began to speak in a ringing voice: "Oh, men of the Abenaki and Mohegan tribes, I come to you with a glorious message from our mighty commander in chief, Sieur de la Salle, the great explorer. I have much to say to you and I want you to understand every word. And so Chief Thunder Hawk," here he bowed to the buffalo-robed figure at his right, "will act as my interpreter. Your ruling chieftain," another bow to Sitting Bear, "tells me that he has lived among the white men and is skilled in the French tongue. So listen well, for the news I bring is most important."

Gabriel understood now why Thunder Hawk sat at the council table, for the Mohegan spoke many languages. Besides, he had a flowing tongue and was deemed a superior orator by his own people. Sometimes there were two interpreters at such conferences, a white man and a red man. But the language of the New England Indians was strange to these parts, so there was no white man there, save Gabriel himself, who could understand both parties to the conference.

Thunder Hawk rose and returned the white chief's bow. He began repeating the other's announcement; only now, Gabriel noticed, all the life was gone out of those ringing words. Instead it sounded dull, halfhearted, and the Indians listened with immobile faces, showing little response.

There was indeed enough to kindle interest in the amazing, yes wonderful, things this stranger went on to tell: "We come to offer you the opportunity to embark on the greatest voyage ever attempted in all the length and breadth of this mighty land."

He flung out his left hand in a wide gesture, his dark face fairly seemed to glow. His whole body was taut and alert save for the gloved right fist that never moved but swung like a dead weight against his side.

Now his flashing eyes passed from face to face, compelling their attention: "Oh, men of the Abenaki, men of the Mohegan, are you brave, are you adventurous? Then listen well, for we will go down the mighty Father of Waters, the great Mississippi River, which flows south until it empties into the sea. You will live forever in the annals of red men and white, for no man has dared what we will dare. You will visit rich, beautiful lands, see strange wonders and enjoy delights you have never known. You will bask in the warm sunshine, feel the soft balmy breezes, for there will be no winter, no ice and snow."

Gabriel felt himself carried away by the power of De Tonti's eloquence. Then suddenly he was startled to hear Thunder Hawk say: "This man wants you to go with him on a long and terrible voyage into the unknown. He says he is going down the great river called the Mississippi. I have heard of that mighty river. He says that it flows south until it reaches the sea. But I have heard different, for no man has ever returned from its fatal waters. Do you know where it empties, oh my brothers? Into the depths of the earth—down, down to the bottomless pit!"

The impassive faces of the red men were coming alive but not with the kind of emotion expected by the whites. There were startled looks, uneasy mutterings, and Gabriel saw a grim little smile playing around Medicine Snake's thin lips. He wondered if Captain de Tonti had any suspicion of what was going on. If so his next words did not betray it, for he started telling about the Chevalier de la Salle; how generous and noble and fearless he was; how he protected and watched over his men like a loving father. He nodded toward the older man—the surgeon, Dr. Jean Michel—sitting near him at the table, and explained that he was a fine medicine man who would take good care of them if they fell sick. He waved toward Father Zenobius who, he said, would look after their souls with tender care. He turned to the clerk at his side, ready with pen and paper to sign them up for the voyage. They would, he promised, receive the highest wages; moreover, the Sieur de la Salle of his own free will always rewarded good and loyal service with extra gifts and pay.

He paused then for Thunder Hawk, to translate. Gabriel already knew too well the Mohegan's treachery, but even so he was shocked at what he heard next: "This man would have you believe that his master is strong and valiant and can save you from all danger. But look at him, my brothers, look and beware. For what manner of master does he serve who sends a weak and helpless cripple as his messenger? A man whose right arm is made of wood?"

There was a long moment of stunned silence, so still Gabriel could hear his own heart thumping like a war drum against his ribs. Then came uproar: red men on their feet, yelling, pointing at the man with the gloved hand, pushing around him.

Gabriel shoved his way through the crowd and, standing boldly before Thunder Hawk, he faced the men at the table. Above the guttural voices of the Indians, he shouted, loud and clear in French: "Thunder Hawk has put false words in the white man's mouth. He talks against the expedition. He tells only of terrible dangers, for he would turn brave men into cowards and make them tremble with fear of the unknown."

De Tonti sprang from his chair. He looked at the boy's quivering face and beyond to the swarming throng. "So that's what's wrong! Tell me what more the knave said, for it's plain he has lied about me, too."

Gabriel's gaze shifted uneasily but he spoke out honestly. "He says you are not a fit leader for men to follow, sir. He says you are only a helpless cripple with a wooden arm."

Fearfully, almost, Gabriel waited to see the effect of the hurtful slur. The man began to smile, showing teeth that were dazzlingly white in his dark face. His snapping black eyes were smiling, too. "So my arm is made of wood! I cannot defend myself," he said quietly. "Well, we shall see."

With the speed of a panther he vaulted across the table and faced the amazed red men. "Tell them," he said to Gabriel and now his voice was strong and defiant, "that I challenge this man who says my arm is made of wood. Ask Thunder Hawk if he is willing to meet me in hand-to-hand combat?"

A fierce surge of pride swept over Gabriel as he translated the challenge. In Thunder Hawk's beady eyes he saw the raging hatred for himself, the withering scorn for the white man. And he glared back with reckless defiance into the savage face.

DiTonti lifted his gloved fist.

Snarling like a wolf, the chief flung off his buffalo skin and advanced on the challenger. He was gigantic, with a thick bull neck and bulging naked torso. The other was younger and nimbler but only of medium height, and when he stripped off his coat, showing his fine linen shirt, the contrast seemed all in the red man's favor.

Silence, taut with suspense, vibrated through the fort. The onlookers pushed back to form a ring for the fighters. Thunder Hawk lunged with fury and confidence for his adversary's weak spot, that sagging right shoulder. But De Tonti sprang away and the fight was on.

Again Thunder Hawk centered his mad charge at De Tonti's shoulder, determined to splinter that dangling arm with one crushing blow and end the struggle. As he crouched for the attack, the white man lifted his gloved hand high, high above his head and held it there, poised and waiting. The big Indian rushed blindly at him and with calm, almost deliberate timing the fist crashed down on Thunder Hawk's skull.

The chief fell to the floor and rolled over and over, screaming in agony. Blood gushed from his head, his face was covered with gore. The white man stepped back. He had struck only one blow; he was cool, unruffled, and it was all over.

He turned to Gabriel. "Ask them now if they think my hand is made of wood."

"No, no," came an outcry from all over the big room. "It is an iron hand."

"With a single stroke of this hand I could have split Chief Thunder Hawk's skull in two. But I did not want to kill him, for I come to you, our sworn allies, with good will and peaceful intentions. I had to wound him to defend myself and prove to you I am no weakling. Now think over what you have seen and heard today and we shall talk again."

Chapter 2

AT FORT ST. JOSEPH

After all had gone and the groaning Mohegan was helped away, the man with the iron hand spoke warmly to his young interpreter. "I am greatly in your debt, my boy," he said with his flashing smile.

As they spoke, Father Zenobius joined them and briefly explained Gabriel's situation.

"I am indeed lucky to find a loyal French boy among the Abenakis," De Tonti remarked. "To think that I should have had to trust that two-faced scoundrel as my interpreter!"

"I speak their language better than my own, sir," Gabriel told him.

De Tonti nodded. "Young as you are, Gabriel, I believe you are able to take Thunder Hawk's place in our conferences here, and I know now I can trust you."

"You can depend on me, sir," the boy promised with all his heart.

After a brief consultation they decided to have Gabriel move into the barracks at the fort. "It will be safer for you here until this storm blows over," De Tonti told him. "Father Zenobius says the pagan Indians resent the Christians bitterly. That's the real reason behind Thunder Hawk's treachery, for of course that villainous old medicine man thought up the whole scheme. They'll blame you for their defeat and your life will be in danger."

Gabriel was delighted to move into the fort with the white men. "I'll have to go back to the village for my things," he said, "and I want to tell my friends. But I'm not afraid—not after today."

Despite himself, Gabriel was staring at the deadly gloved hand; somehow his eyes kept coming back to it.

Not at all embarrassed by Gabriel's boyish curiosity, De Tonti held up the artificial member. "The Iroquois call me Iron Hand, but this hand is really of bronze, made by the finest metal craftsmen in Paris. Several years ago when I was fighting with the French in Sicily my hand was blown away by a Spanish grenade," he explained quite casually. "I learned to shoot and fence with my left hand and this-one serves me as well as a tomahawk."

"Ah, how cool and unconcerned you sound, my gallant Henri," exclaimed the friar. "You did not tell our young friend that at the time you speak of you were in command of a force of 20,000 troops at Messina, that you were taken prisoner and held captive for six months, nor that when you were finally exchanged for the son of the Spanish governor on your return to France you were rewarded by the King for your heroism. And after that, Gabriel, he went right back to the fighting in Sicily as a volunteer in the galleys—the only way a man with a handicap like his could re-enlist in the King's service."

De Tonti laughed off the friar's words. "Soldiering, adventuring—that's my whole life, Father, so I *had* to turn my handicap into an advantage. Every military man knows that a battle is not lost if one refuses to accept defeat."

What a man to follow, Gabriel was thinking as he hurried away to the village. Breathless and excited, he burst into the long house where he lived with François Black Otter and his numerous kinfolk. It was this goodhearted Christian Indian and his wife who had taken him in and reared him with their own family. All their children were grown now and married, and lived in separate apartments in the long house. These opened on a middle passage, and here and there were fireplaces which they shared for cooking. Gabriel felt at home with all of Black Otter's family.

Already the oldest grandson, Petit Jean Brown Beaver, who was eighteen, was pleading to join the expedition. And Black Otter's youngest son, Vincent Running Elk, was in the midst of a family argument. He was twenty-four and the father of a three-year-old son; his wife thought he should either stay home or take them with him.

They all began at once to help Gabriel pack his belongings to take to the fort. There wasn't very much besides his warm robe of beaver skins, for his possessions were few: an extra shirt and breeches of deerskin, a belt trimmed with bright-hued pebbles, a stone hatchet and knife, some armlets and a neckband made of the polished ribs of the deer, a few trinkets, and the rosary he wore about his neck.

"And here are your bows and arrows, White Moose," said Brown Beaver, calling Gabriel by his tribal name as was the custom even among the baptized Indians. "I wish *you* were old enough to go on this great expedition."

Gabriel hadn't thought about the bows and arrows, for he was planning something better—something he never would have dared to attempt before today. There was a grim little smile on his young face as he walked away with his pack on his back. Going in the opposite direction from the fort, he headed for the lodge of the once-mighty Chief Thunder Hawk.

Long had the big Mohegan bullied him, but then he had been a child with a child's fears and a child's helpless submission to his elders. Today he had defied Thunder Hawk and fearlessly unmasked him before all the people. He had done it in the heat of anger and to right a wrong against one of his own race. White Moose, the stripling, had confounded the great chief.

Thunder Hawk was lying on a pile of furs, nursing his bandaged head. There was no one attending him but his wife—which was to be expected after his disgrace. They looked up in surprise when he came in and the stricken chief grunted and tried to rise, then fell back with a groan.

Gabriel walked over to the comer where the long-barreled firelock was propped against the wall. "I've come for my father's gun," he said. That was all. He picked the weapon up and flung it over his shoulder and strode away without a backward glance. There was no sound, no movement in the place.

That night at the barracks Gabriel learned more about the Chevalier de Tonti. Lying on his beaver robe near the fireplace he listened eagerly to the talk that went around among the men. Great logs blazed on the hearth, lighting up their faces as they sprawled at ease before turning in for the night.

There was the young man who had acted as clerk at the meeting. He was Lieutenant Louis de Boisrondet, a close friend and great admirer of the captain. They'd shared many adventures in the three years since De Tonti had come from France with the Sieur de la Salle. And there was his sublieutenant, Jean Couture, also in his twenties. Like La Salle himself he was a Norman and came from the same city of Rouen. Both these young men were lean, broad-shouldered, all bone, brawn and sinew. They were the skilled, intrepid forest rangers who were known as the *coureurs de bois.*

The other newcomer, Pierre Prudhomme, was a heavyweight with round china blue eyes and flaxen hair. He was not long away from a Breton farm, and since he had been a great hunter and fisher back home, he was quite sure he could take care of himself in this wild new world.

Father Zenobius, the surgeon Dr. Jean Michel, and Captain de Tonti were lodged in separate quarters and Gabriel was glad, since it gave his companions the opportunity to talk freely about the fascinating dark man with the iron hand. He was not surprised to learn that De Tonti was an Italian, the son of a Neapolitan banker who had invented a form of insurance called the Tontine. The elder Tonti had fled to Paris as a refugee after taking a prominent part in the Neapolitan revolt against Spain in 1649. It was around that time that Henri was born. The boy had been educated in France and at sixteen had enlisted as a cadet in the French army.

"La Salle never had a truer friend nor a braver follower in the whole world than Henri de Tonti," Boisrondet said warmly. "I remember the time a handful of us were staying among the Illinois at their Kaskaskia village on the north bank of the Illinois River. A war party of some six hundred Iroquois braves decended on them and threw them into a panic. We assured them we'd fight with them, but we were only five, and one was our good Father Zenobius. Our friends were outnumbered two to three."

"Even if they were equal the Illinois would be no match for those bloodthirsty fiends," Sergeant Ako put in.

The lieutenant nodded. "That we knew. Well, De Tonti hadn't been in this country too long and wasn't too well acquainted with their manners, so he rashly decided to go and treat with the enemy singlehanded."

Couture chuckled. "I've heard Commandant la Salle say never let yourself fear even if you're alone against a thousand. De Tonti must have taken that advice to the letter."

"He did indeed, for armed only with a handful of presents—necklaces I believe they were—he walked right into the Iroquois camp. As soon as he got within range they opened fire. The bullets missed and De Tonti, waving the necklaces to show his peaceful intentions, went right ahead. They overpowered him, grabbed the peace offerings and one of the braves plunged a knife in his breast—"

"Ah, that was a close call for our daring captain," broke in the Picard.

"Luckily for him the blade lodged in a rib and missed his heart. But perhaps Father Zenobius' prayers had something to do with that," Boisrondet added with a smile. "Anyway, the Iroquois saw they'd made a mistake and this wasn't an Illinois but a white man. So they took him to their chief for questioning.

"Tonti didn't know their language but he managed to make them understand. He told them that the Illinois were under the protection of the governor of New France and that he was surprised they should make war on a nation that was allied to the Sieur de la Salle.

"While this was going on a warrior burst in with the bad news that Frenchmen had been seen fighting with the Illinois. This made the chiefs so angry that they turned against De Tonti and held a council to decide whether to kill him. One of the Iroquois, the chief of the Onondagas, was a friend of La Salle and wanted to spare De Tonti for that reason, but the Seneca chief was all for burning him at the stake.

He waved the necklace to show his peaceful intentions.

"It was a harrowing session, for a murderous savage stood over the captain with a knife, and, when the debate turned against him, he'd yank De Tonti's hair up and get ready to scalp him. And all the time he was bleeding from the mouth and from his wound. In the end the friendly chief carried his point, and they sent De Tonti back to make peace negotiations with the Illinois.

"But this wasn't the end by any means. After De Tonti was well enough to travel, the tricky Iroquois sent for him and Father Zenobius. When they reached the Iroquois headquarters some miles away, the council members presented them with six packets of fine beaver skins. The first was to inform the governor they would not eat his children—"

Pierre Prudhomme gave a horrified gasp. "But you don't mean these Iroquois are cannibals?"

"But certainly they eat their prisoners," broke out Ako. "They're devils, I tell you. They take the greatest delight in torturing them for days."

"Terrible, terrible," exclaimed the round-eyed Breton with a shudder. "It's hard to believe there is such cruelty even among the savages."

"The sergeant isn't exaggerating, my friend," went on Boisrondet grimly. "The Iroquois boast of devouring a nation a year; they actually feast on the flesh of captured enemies, dead or alive. It takes a strong man like Iron Hand to put the fear of God into them, let me tell you. Well, to get back to my story—the wily rascals then offered De Tonti the rest of the beaver packets; the second to ask his forgiveness for almost killing him, the third as a sort of plaster for his wound, the fourth as a soothing oil to be rubbed on his and his companion's limbs which must be weary and aching after their journey. The fifth and sixth packets were to point out that the sun was shining brightly and the Frenchmen ought to take advantage of the good weather and leave the next morning.

"Instead of accepting the gifts, De Tonti asked when they intended to clear out. 'Not until we've eaten some of the Illinois,' was the answer. At that De Tonti scornfully kicked away their presents, saying he would have none of them.

"The chiefs rose up and drove him and Father Zenobius from the council. They were furious and we thought surely they'd slaughter us—since the Illinois meanwhile had abandoned their village. Instead, they allowed us to depart in peace."

"There's one thing you have to say for them," Couture observed; "they admire and respect a courageous foe."

Long after the others were sound asleep, Gabriel lay awake staring into the glowing embers, his mind on fire. Oh, how he wanted to join this expedition and go with these brave men down the mighty Mississippi all the way to the sea! But he was only a boy; they'd never take him. He'd heard Boisrondet say they needed seventeen volunteers to complete La Salle's company, and surely there'd be plenty more than that among the braves who'd want to go.

But Gabriel was mistaken, for despite many conferences in which he acted as interpreter, enlistments were slow. Weeks passed; golden Indian summer turned to bleak November, the winds blew cold, the earth lay blackened by the frost. Before they knew it, winter would be upon them and any day now the Sieur de la Salle was expected to arrive at St. Joseph's with his forces to start on the great voyage.

A few at a time the Indians enlisted; finally there were six unmarried braves ranging from seventeen to twenty years old, and ten married men who agreed to go if they were allowed to take their wives. When this was permitted, three small children had to be added; their mothers refused to go without them.

"That makes twenty-nine in all, Captain," Gabriel heard Boisrondet telling De Tonti one morning early in December. "We're still short a man."

Hope and fear tugged at Gabriel's heart. "Won't you take me, sir?" he asked De Tonti. "I'll be sixteen in February. I can shoot and handle a canoe, do anything the others can. And I could load your pistols for you."

De Tonti's face lit up in one of his dazzling smiles. "Sixteen—just my age when I enlisted in the army as a cadet."

Gabriel's eyes were shining. "Then you mean I can go— you'll take me on the expedition—" the words came tumbling out.

De Tonti studied him a moment. "If you are sure you want to come along—"

"Oh, sir, I never wanted anything so much in my life."

Impulsively Gabriel reached out and grasped the iron hand.

A look passed between the captain and his clerk. Boisrondet was smiling too as he nodded his approval.

"You'll do, Gabriel. You'll do," said De Tonti.

Chapter 3

THE FATHER OF WATERS

December was well advanced before Commandant de la Salle arrived at Fort St. Joseph. With him were such trusted and able comrades as Captain d'Autray, son of the first procurer general of Quebec; the scholarly Jacques de la Metairie, official notary; and the faithful Shawnee hunter, Nica, whom La Salle had purchased as a war prisoner twelve years before. Nica had never left his master since, even accompanying him on two trips to France.

La Salle found everything ready for the expedition: the Indian escort, which with his own men brought the party to fifty-four; the supplies; the ten stout, well-constructed canoes they would travel in. Each canoe was twenty feet long and built of birchwood so light that a man could carry one by himself but was strong enough to bear with ease a crew of four and eight hundred pounds of baggage.

"Well done, Captain," La Salle told De Tonti when the two met to discuss their plans. "We should be loaded by day after tomorrow, should we not? We can start at once."

"This brings us to December 21, the first day of winter," De Tonti observed gravely.

"A late start, I know, but this time nothing can stop us."

La Salle was pacing up and down the small room, a towering six feet and a half in his military boots, with great rugged shoulders—a man of the wilderness yet an aristocrat with chiseled features and an air of natural dignity and pride.

De Tonti shared the driving impatience of his chief, for this was their third attempt to explore the Mississippi. The first two had ended in failure and disaster, but reverses had only sharpened the will to succeed in these two resolute men.

"This time we shall not be stopped by Indian wars as we were a year and a half ago, my Commandant. The strong alliance you have built up between the Illinois tribes now protects them from the Iroquois raiders."

"I couldn't have done that without your help, Captain. While I was smoking peace pipes and feasting with the Illinois and the Miamis and the Shawnees, you valiantly drove the enemy from their villages."

It was true, each had done his part to make the Illinois country a safe place for their Indian allies. Otherwise, as both realized, even if the great voyage of discovery were successful, it would actually lead nowhere. For behind La Salle's glorious dream of traveling the great inland water route from Canada to the Gulf was his plan to settle the Mississippi Valley and claim a vast new empire for France—a land where colonist and native might dwell together in peace and prosperity.

"We have indeed shared many adventures," said De Tonti, "since that summer's day in Paris in 1678—four years ago— when the Prince de Conty brought me to you at the French Court and asked that I be permitted to accompany you back to New France. I'll never forget the occasion—I was very nervous and feared my handicap would ruin my chances for enlistment with the great La Salle."

La Salle ceased his restless pacing and sat down facing his aide. "You needn't have feared, Henri. The moment you walked into the room, I knew you were the man I was looking for. And you have surpassed my highest hopes, you know. . . ." Then he added in lighter vein: "Besides, isn't it true, Chief Iron Hand, that it is your famous metal fist that has won so much respect for us among the Iroquois?"

He was speaking with unusual warmth, for he was a reserved person with few intimates. But in the company of Henri de Tonti he was more at ease than with anyone he had ever known.

La Salle had been only twenty-three when he came to New France, as Canada was called, in 1666. An older brother, the Abbé Jean Cavelier, was a priest of the Sulpician Society in Montreal and for three years the younger man stayed on a small estate given him by the Sulpicians near the settlement. He had mastered seven or eight different languages and even then dreamed of a vast inland waterway that would connect the French settlements in Canada with the Gulf of Mexico.

In the summer of 1669, La Salle started out on a voyage that led to his discovery of the Ohio River. Two years later he was back in Montreal preparing for another expedition that ended in the discovery of the Illinois River. Then in 1673 Père Marquette, the Jesuit missionary to the Indians, and Louis Jolliet, the Canadian-born explorer and fur trader, starting out from Lake Michigan, had found the Mississippi and had voyaged down it as far south as the Arkansas River.

It took five years of preparation before La Salle's own first expedition to explore the Mississippi got under way.

Meanwhile he had made two trips to France to obtain from King Louis XIV the authority to build military forts and trading posts and to continue the explorations of Marquette and Joliet in the name of the Crown. It was on the second of these trips that he met the young Chevalier de Tonti who had seen eight years of wartime service on land and sea and who had come to him highly recommended for courage and ability.

"How anxious I was to sign up with you that day, my Commandant," De Tonti went on, smiling over the memory of that first meeting. "The wars at home had quieted down, I was at loose ends. But more than that was the urge for adventure and discovery in the strange New World across the ocean."

A more serious look came over his dark, expressive face; his eyes revealed the depth of his feeling. "And then you brought me back with you to this great, wonderful, wild country, placed me second in command, even put me in charge of building the *Griffin*. Ah, what a goodly ship that was—"

He broke off abruptly, for even now the strange disappearance of that magnificent vessel was painful to dwell upon. Several years before La Salle had sent his trusted aide to a point above Niagara Falls to construct a fortified trading post and build a large sailboat that could easily pass through the Great Lakes and sail to the mouth of the St. Joseph River. It was the first and most important move in his carefully planned preparations for the Mississippi venture.

The forty-five-ton schooner De Tonti had built and launched on the Niagara River was the wonder and envy of all, red men and white, for never had a ship like the *Griffin* been seen in the Lake country. They took note of her five cannon and called her "the floating fort." And many speculated about her cost to La Salle and his backers, which was all of 10,000 écus, equal to 30,000 livres or dollars.

Proudly the wonder ship had navigated Lakes Erie and Huron and reached Lake Michigan. And there during an equinoctial storm in September, 1679, she just seemed to have been swallowed up. Mysterious, baffling disaster, for none of her crew of six picked seamen ever returned to tell what had happened. Nothing was ever seen or heard of the *Griffin* again. Lost too was her precious cargo, worth 12,000 livres. Thus all the supplies La Salle had collected for his expedition were sunk: merchandise, ammunitions, supplies and tools—thousands upon thousands of pounds of valuables that could not be replaced.

"My enemies thought I was done for then," La Salle's voice broke in on De Tonti's reverie. "Well-meaning friends, too, urged me to give up the Mississippi exploration and go back to Fort Frontenac on Lake Ontario. As the commandant there I was assured a fine profit—25,000 livres a year. My reverend brother was among the most insistent."

De Tonti gave a short laugh. "Not the life for you, sir. You lack the trader's instinct."

"I've never sought money for its own sake," his chief agreed. "I want to serve my country worthily, and the more perilous and hardy the undertaking, the more it appeals to me."

He rose, ending their conference. "And now before we set out I must have a talk with Father Zenobius."

When the expedition set out from Fort St. Joseph on December 21st, winter had overtaken them, and all the waterways were solid sheets of ice. They had to make sledges for their canoes and drag them across the frozen surface of

Lake Michigan to the Illinois River where, on the last day of January, 1682, they finally reached open water.

At the head of the long string of canoes rode La Salle, and in the second boat De Tonti with young Gabriel La Grue beside him. Very much a part of the group was Father Zenobius, for he and La Salle were very close. La Salle would no more have started on a journey without a priest than he would without food and ammunition. Each morning when they embarked for the day they knelt in prayer, and when darkness came they said their night prayers around their campfire. Father Zenobius carried his portable altar with him so that he could celebrate Mass every Sunday.

Now the canoes were gliding swiftly along, carried downstream by a rapid current. A stiff wind was blowing

La Salle rode in the first canoe.

from the northeast and it was cold—intensely cold. But they were following the sun, moving ever westward. The woods dwindled, broad plains stretched away under fleecy blankets of snow.

One day flowed into the next and now their course was dipping almost due south. The scene changed, flat lands rolled up in pine-clad slopes of deepest emerald. The dark woods came down to the shore. The river widened and its tide grew much faster; their small craft shot onward like arrows. Only the skill of the men at the paddles kept them from being swept away, for they were rushing down, down to the mouth of the Illinois.

Suddenly the forest seemed to be alive with waters; before them rolled an immense flood that looked miles and miles across. They could understand now why the Indians had named it the Mississippi, for this must indeed be the Father of All the Waters. These men—white as well as red—were used to the majestic grandeur of vast solitudes and nature's wild beauty, but nothing they had ever seen prepared them for a river of this size.

The paddles idled, the boats lay afloat as they gazed and gazed. And looking around at the different faces, Gabriel could see the reflection of his own feelings: wonder and elation and a kind of solemn joy. Then a ringing cheer went up and echoed far across the waters to come rolling back from the distant shores. They had reached the Mississippi. It was almost noon on February 6 in this memorable year of 1682.

Then the canoes were out on the broad bosom of the deep, slow-moving Father of Waters. The voyage into the unknown was under way.

The party guided their boats toward the western shore where the current was making about three miles an hour. "We should cover eighteen miles easily before the sun goes down," Captain de Tonti said.

Gabriel didn't feel like talking, it was so thrilling to be paddling down the big river. He watched the winter sunlight playing over its clear waters and the wind rippling them in gentle waves, and here and there the islands rising from its surface, some large, some small. The fish were jumping, and now and then a flight of birds whirred up from the thick forest that grew right down to the bank.

Eighteen miles downstream they halted before the rushing waters of a great tawny river that poured a torrent of mud, uprooted trees and drifted timber into the Mississippi. This was the mighty Missouri, the Father of Nations, so-called by the red men because of the numerous western tribes that dwelt near its long and winding banks. It gushed into the clean waters, miring them from shore to shore, turning the Mississippi into a river of gold.

The men slept that night at the mouth of the Missouri, and with the dawn crossed over to the eastern shore. They went on to the village of the Tamaroas, an Illinois tribe, eighteen miles off, but found no one there as the Indians had moved to their winter quarters in the woods. After making marks with their axes on the trees to inform the Tamaroas they had passed, they went on downstream as far as the mouth of the Ohio, 240 miles southeast of the Illinois.

Food was not a problem at this stage of the journey. The river yielded enormous catfish, and on the shore the men hunted buffalo, deer, turkey and other birds. But when the rainy season set in, the river rose, and it became difficult to land and look for food on the sodden lowlands along the river. They had begun to run low on provisions when one day the party was relieved to see a range of high bluffs rising above the swampland along the eastern shore.

It was February 24 and the sun was beginning to shine again after the depressing days of dismal weather. The high open country looked inviting, and the broad meadows of tall dried grass obviously afforded good winter grazing for buffalo. La Salle decided that the site looked promising for a hunt and gave the order to land at the next bluff.

"I'm going to volunteer for the hunt," spoke up Pierre Prudhomme as they landed. "I want to bring down one of those huge wild oxen myself. They look frightening with their monstrous heads and long black hair, but they don't seem to mind when a man comes near."

"Don't let Mr. Buffalo fool you," Jean Couture advised. "He can't see with that bush falling into his eyes, but his hearing and smell are so keen they make up for it. Be sure you go against the wind and take good aim. Don't just wound him, for he'll charge with blind fury and then you're in trouble."

The round-faced Breton nodded sagely. "I shall do exactly as you say, Lieutenant. One direct hit at the hollow of the shoulder and *voilá*, he is down! Ah, we shall feast like princes! Never in France have I tasted a dish that could compare to that hunch on the back of the North American ox."

"I've eaten so much buffalo meat, I feel as though I've grown a hump myself," Martin de Launay said with a chuckle. He was from Rouen like Couture and the two had been friends from boyhood. "But I'm hungry enough to eat anything—even a mitchybitchy."

Pierre looked startled; they ate such awful things in this strange new land. "Mitchybitchy, what's that?"

"You tell him, Father Zenobius," said Martin, laughing. "I haven't the eloquence to describe the beast."

The friar was shaking his head. "The mitchybitchy is nothing to joke about. I don't want to alarm you, Pierre, but you should know what it looks like so you'll recognize it if you meet one. I'd say it's a cross between a lion and a leopard. It has the lion's tawny coat and the long thick tail but no mane and it isn't as large. The head and ears resemble the leopard, and it has large paws with very long strong claws. It's a flesh-eater but preys mostly on smaller animals and birds."

"Then it wouldn't attack a human?" Pierre asked.

"Usually not unless it is aroused or infuriated," Martin explained. "Mitchybitchy is the Indian name. It's very similar to our cougar—anyway it belongs to the family of big cats and I wouldn't want to meet one unarmed."

"Come along with me, Gabriel," said Pierre as the hunting party was getting under way. "You're just a boy but you're a born hunter like these Indians, and I've never seen a white man with your skill at the bow and arrow. You can handle firearms, besides."

"Oh, I don't know much about a gun but I'm learning all the time."

Pierre cast an appraising eye over the boy's firelock. "That was a good gun in its day but it goes back a long way. Too slow and awkward to operate. Now this flintlock I have is the most up-to-date thing. It shoots from the shoulder and has a trigger instead of that obsolete S-shaped match-holder they call the serpentine."

"You know a lot about guns, Pierre," said Gabriel admiringly but a little wistfully. Up ahead were the boy's old friends Brown Beaver and Running Elk and he would have liked to join them. But he had to slow his pace to that of the chubby Frenchman.

Pierre was puffing when they reached the bluff, though the distance wasn't more than half a mile. "That was a steep climb, Gabriel, and now that we're here I don't see any buffalo."

"Most likely they smelled us and ran away. But they've been here. See that trail?" And Gabriel pointed to a wide path of trampled grass.

They moved along in an easterly direction, where the open meadow was crossed by a tall grove of trees. Here the partridges rose up in droves at their footfall.

"Ah, how I'd like to have a nice fat pair of you in a skillet," cried Pierre, his mouth watering at the idea. "A few bay leaves, a dash of garlic and the chefs of Paris would throw away their cookbooks in envy."

Gabriel was laughing heartily. "You'll never catch them now, Pierre. Besides, I thought you wanted to kill a buffalo."

"Of course, but I'm growing weak from lack of food."

They hadn't gone far when the Breton gave a cry and pointed to the bare branches of a tall cottonwood. "Oh, what a queer little beast!"

Hanging head down by its long hairless tail was something that looked like a ball of gray fur. Its eyes were shut tight and it seemed to be either sound asleep or dead. When they moved closer it did not stir.

"Now what do you call that creature?" Pierre asked. "It's about the size of a large cat and those big paws have long, sharp claws. The head and tail resemble a rat, but it has a snout and it's round and fat like a pig."

"It's called an opossum," Gabriel explained, "and it's delicious. The Indians roast it with a kind of potato known as a yam, yellow and sweet as sugar."

His words were evidently too much for Pierre, for much to Gabriel's surprise the Breton swung his musket to his shoulder, took aim and fired. The strange little animal hit the ground with a thump, killed instantly by the bullet through its head.

Pierre pulled his knife from his belt and began skinning it. "I've never eaten one of these," he told Gabriel with a laugh, "and I'm going to find out what it tastes like."

"Don't you think we ought to wait until we get back to camp where there's a fire?"

Pierre brushed aside the question with a wave of the hand. "We can start a fire here in no time and broil ourselves a slice or two or three on the end of a stick. Who knows? As you say, it may be delicious, and anyway, as hungry as I am, it doesn't matter."

But Gabriel was restive, and through the tree trunks he saw the flash of a red-brown body. Pierre's shot had startled a deer.

"Go ahead if you must, my impatient nimrod," said the Breton, seeing the boy's impatience. "I'll join you at the camp."

But sometime later, when Gabriel returned to camp with the fine deer he had killed, he learned that Pierre had not arrived. After a while all the others came back, bringing their catch of buffalo and smaller game. They feasted on broiled slices of turkey meat while the main meal was being prepared. And still Pierre did not return.

"He can't be far away," said Gabriel confidently, and he told them how the hungry Breton had stopped to eat only a short distance from where they had started. They laughed over it, agreeing that he would be back before nightfall. "Perhaps after eating he fell asleep in the forest," Captain de Tonti surmised.

But then before they noticed, the winter sun was sinking across the river, shadows began creeping over the lonely bluffs, while down in the swampy woods the mists were rising. It was growing cold and dark. But still no sign of Pierre Prudhomme.

"Keep the fires banked all night so their light may guide him," said La Salle and his face looked very grave. "Set a guard around the camp, Captain de Tonti. We'll start the search at daybreak."

For two days they beat the countryside, but only the echoes of their own anxious cries came back from the great lonely spaces. La Salle sent out searching parties in every direction, most of them made up of Indians. They were experts in reading the wilderness signs, and besides he needed his own men to help Captain de Tonti in building a fort.

This fort was a very primitive, rapid piece of construction: just a log house with a stockade built of uprights but affording some protection in case they should be attacked by hostile natives. Here in the privacy of their makeshift headquarters, La Salle and De Tonti felt free to show the anxiety they hid from their company.

"I'm badly worried over Prudhomme," La Salle was saying as dusk began to fall at the end of that second day.

De Tonti's face was as unhappy as his chiefs. "I know, Commandant. What a misfortune! And we've had such good luck until this—"

He broke off at the sound of running feet, of voices outside. They sprang up, hope and relief lifting their hearts.

But it was only Nica with Gabriel. "We found this, master, under a tree near the place where Pierre was last seen."

It was Pierre's flintlock. La Salle took it and sat down heavily on the crude bench. "We know what this means," he told De Tonti with a sigh, for to lose his weapon was the worst thing that could befall a man alone in the wilderness.

"We'll find him, Commandant," De Tonti cried resolutely. "I'll go myself in the morning."

"Then take Nica with you, Henri," said La Salle. "And bring the Breton back—dead or alive. We won't leave until he's found, no matter how long the delay."

Chapter 4

THE HORRIBLE MITCHY-
BITCHY

Gabriel was grateful to be chosen as one of Captain de Tonti's search party, for he blamed himself bitterly for what had happened. He should never have left Pierre alone in the forest; he had come only recently from his native France, and had no real experience in the wilderness.

Besides Nica, the best scout in the company, and Gabriel, the others in the party were Chief Little Wolf, Brown Beaver and a young Frenchman named Giles Renault, who had enlisted with Captain de Tonti at Paris when he was only eighteen.

It was Giles who made a startling discovery. They had traveled many miles since morning and had come to a stream with a dense thicket of cane along its borders. Suddenly the young Frenchman shrank back, his eyes staring in terror, his face pallid under its coat of tan.

"Did you see that?" he managed to ask in a hoarse whisper. "Over there on the other bank—a horrible face—"

"What do you mean?" asked the captain sharply. "Was it a human or an animal?"

Renault shuddered. "It's human, I think, sir, though I never saw a face that size—larger than a big soup plate—and the head was flat. Oh, it must be one of those terrible monsters we heard about—half beast, half man."

"What nonsense!" said De Tonti. "Pull yourself together, man, and we'll soon find out what it is."

The red men were glancing uneasily at each other; human beings like themselves could not frighten them but unknown monsters struck terror to the bravest hearts. Even the valiant Nica hung back and let the captain take the lead.

With the caution of a frontier soldier, De Tonti moved silently toward the canebrakes and peered across the bank. "I see nothing—nothing at all," he announced positively. "Renault, I'm afraid your imagination has been playing tricks on you. Monsters with flat heads and soup-plate faces—"

"Someone was there, Captain," said Nica quietly. "Behold—" and he pointed to a flock of birds that had flown up from the other bank.

"We'll take after him, then. But remember, men, you are not to attack. Never make the first hostile move no matter who—or what—it is. That's our Commandant's order. Nica, I want you to go ahead and study the ground for signs."

Cautiously the Shawnee scout waded the stream and began examining the bank. He looked up and he was smiling with relief as he pointed to an imprint in the mud. "These are the marks of moccasins," he said. "They are red men like ourselves."

"Then we must find them," said De Tonti. "They've probably captured our poor Pierre so we'll have to treat them in a very friendly way."

Gabriel's heart felt lighter than it had since the Breton disappeared. Oh, if only he could be the one to find Pierre! He kept close to Nica, scanning the brush and the trampled grass for clues. They were nearing the open meadows when they saw them—two figures lurking at the foot of a sloping hill.

He crouched back in the underbrush, signaling to the others. They kept their distance as they quickly decided what to do next. "I'll go, Captain," Nica volunteered. "I have some knowledge of the languages of the southern nations."

"Be careful then," De Tonti cautioned. "Better go unarmed. We'll keep you covered."

They watched the Shawnee moving boldly toward the strange pair, saw him holding up his hands in the peace signal, making the signs of friendship and good will. They held their breath and waited to see what the savages would do. And then, to their joy, they saw them returning the peace signs, shaking hands with Nica.

"There are your monsters, Giles," said the captain, laughing heartily in relief. "And I can't blame you much, for these are the ugliest, queerest-looking natives I have ever seen. Look at those heads—flat as a board."

Nica relied more on the universal sign language of the red men than he did on his smattering knowledge of their tongue to make his message clear to the hideous pair. By promising them all sorts of gifts he quickly induced them to come with him to the great white chieftain who had just arrived on the shores. The Sieur de la Salle, Nica assured them, had only love and the most benevolent intentions toward the people who dwelt along the mighty Mississippi.

"They are Chickasaws," Nica told his companions on the way back to the fort. "Their village is three days' journey from the river and they are out hunting for a pair of escaped war prisoners—valuable hostages, the young son and daughter of the chieftain of the great Quapaw nation that dwells to the south on the western banks of the Mississippi and along the Arkansas River."

"Why, that's where Jolliet and Father Marquette ended their voyage of discovery," De Tonti recalled. "One cannot help but wonder how much farther they would have had to go to reach the sea. Perhaps it was fear that made them turn back, but they were indeed brave to venture so far as they did with such a small company and so little equipment."

The Chickasaws had never seen a white man before so they were as startled in their own way as were La Salle and his company when the moon-faced flatheads were brought into the fort.

"We'll hold one for a hostage," the Commandant decided, "and send the other back under escort to make a trade for Prudhomme if they've captured him and are holding him at their village."

Gabriel wanted to go along but Captain de Tonti shook his head. "You're worn out, my boy. This time I'm taking Captain Boisrondet and some fresh men."

However, it again seemed wise to include Nica in the party not only because he could make himself understood but also because he had won the confidence of the strange pair. How their black eyes glistened when he showed them the flashy trading goods, all the bright gaudy objects that the red people loved: beads, finger rings, bracelets and anklets!

"We must take along plenty of knives and cookware," De Tonti decided. "We can be sure they have no steel or iron utensils, and they'll really value them."

De Tonti asked Father Zenobius to look after Gabriel while he was gone. "He's only a boy, Father, and he's letting this prey on his mind, I'm afraid."

"Yes, I've noticed the drawn look on his face," the priest said. "Don't worry, Henri, I'll keep an eye on him. But it's going to be an anxious time for us all while you're away."

The messengers could not be expected back for six days: three to reach the Chickasaw village and three to return. Meanwhile, at the fort the hunt elsewhere for Pierre was not abandoned, since there was always the possibility that he had not been picked up by the Indians. But as the days went by without a vestige of the missing Breton, the belief became stronger that he would be found at the Chickasaw village.

As they waited Father Zenobius and La Salle occupied themselves in their free moments with a study of the mineral resources of the country, and they located several rich veins of coal and iron. Both were men of learning and interested in science and geology. Gabriel divided his time between hunting for Pierre with his Indian friends and prospecting with Father Zenobius.

It was now the morning of the sixth day since the couriers had left for the village of the Chickasaws and suspense had mounted to a high pitch at the fort. Would they, in just a matter of hours, see their amiable comrade walking in, safe and smiling? Or would the messengers come back without Pierre—ah, what then?

Noticing how tense the boy looked, Father Zenobius placed a kindly hand on Gabriel's shoulder. "Let us combine forces today," he said. "You take your gun and I'll take my axe. And while you hunt, I'll prospect. Something tells me we'll make some discoveries."

Gabriel's face brightened. It was always like that with Father Zenobius; no matter how downhearted and upset you might be, he could make you feel better.

The friar led the way, for he knew exactly where he was headed. It was early March and already the touch of spring was in the breeze fanning their cheeks and in the warbling of the wood thrush. After crossing a wide meadow they passed through a dark grove of scented pines where the thick needles made a soft carpet underfoot.

As they came out of the woods they saw just ahead of them a small hill bare of vegetation except for two stunted oaks. "This is the place I wanted to explore, Gabriel," said the friar with a satisfied air. "There is a cave around on the other side. I'm going to have a look at it."

The mouth of the cave was big enough for Father Zenobius to walk into by stooping a little. Gabriel stayed outside, attracted by a little stream that flowed nearby. He parted the bushes and knelt down beside it to drink, for suddenly he realized he was thirsty. The cool clear water tasted good and he satisfied himself fully; then pulling off his deerhide jacket he dashed handfuls of water over his head and shoulders.

Around his neck was the blue rosary that had been his mother's. Somehow the sight and feel of it brought peace to his spirit—that and the enchantment of nature, the concert of birds filling the thickets, the low music of the brook. He closed his eyes and a grateful prayer welled up from his heart. He felt sure that Pierre would be found, that everything was going to be well.

But just then there broke in on his prayers a frightful sound, a furious, snarling noise. Gabriel whirled and sheer horror turned his blood to ice. There in front of the cave he saw a huge mitchybitchy ready to spring upon Father Zenobius. Its terrible fangs were bared in rage, its long tail lashed in fury.

The friar was ready to defend himself; he had his axe poised for a swing. But Gabriel sensed in a flash that the priest was helpless before the giant cat. One spring of that tremendous body and he would be hurled to the ground and torn to death by those rending, tearing claws.

Gabriel's hands were shaking as he tore off the pan cover and brought the massive stock of his old firelock up against his chest. With one finger he drew back the lower part of the serpentine and for a second his keen eyes sighted down the barrel.

Excited as he was, Gabriel knew he dare not miss. He must strike a vital spot, the first shot must kill, not maim, the infuriated beast. Then a disastrous thing happened— the gun did not go off!

The mitchybitchy slid back on his haunches, ready for the leap. Desperately Gabriel worked the serpentine, but it was useless. The match had failed to ignite. It was true he carried a reserve of powder in a container tied around his gun, but poor Father Zenobius would be torn to pieces before he had time to reload.

And then Gabriel saw a long shaft, feathered at the top, swoop like a darting hawk through the air. Straight it went to its mark—into the head of the lunging beast. Cold sweat broke out over Gabriel. His legs sagged, his shaking hand dropped the gun and it clattered to the ground. He was powerless to move or speak.

The wounded animal bounded into the air, its death howls rising on the wind. Then down it crashed on the exact spot from which it had sprung, and, with paws lashing the air,

rolled on its back. A final struggle, and then all was still.

The thicket parted and an Indian youth, not much older than Gabriel, came forward, his bow strung over his shoulder. He was tall and handsome with very broad shoulders and long black hair and black eyes.

Close behind came a girl of about twelve. She was beautiful, too, with a close resemblance to the youth, save that her eyes were hazel with golden lights. Both young people were smiling, and it was plain to see they were brother and sister.

"I could almost believe them to be angels sent from heaven, Gabriel," said Father Zenobius, his voice trembling from the strain of his experience. "Yet I'm almost sure these must be the escaped prisoners of the Chickasaws."

*The Indian youth sent
his arrow through the air*

By means of the sign language he tried to tell the youth how thankful he was to him for saving his life. As he did so, the young Indian pointed to the crucifix Father Zenobius wore on his breast and to his friar's habit. The girl was pointing, too, and then a most amazing thing happened: she showed them a slender chain of silver with a little silver cross that she was wearing around her neck.

"But how could such a thing be found here?" Gabriel asked in wonder.

In a language that Gabriel could only partly understand but filled in by eloquent signs and meaningful gestures, the Indian youth gave them the answer. Nine years before another man like Father Zenobius—a man who wore the image of the Crucified on his breast and who was dressed in a long black robe—had come to their nation across the Mississippi. The Black Robe, as they called him, was good and kind and told them wonderful things about the Great Spirit in heaven, the Father of all men.

"Father Marquette, Lord rest his soul," the friar said reverently. "I feel that we owe our lives to him, for clearly his teachings live on in these beautiful children."

There was more to the strange, touching story, for now the youth, whose name was Sun Eaglet, was telling them that at the time he was speaking of his sister had been very sick and they had feared she would die. The Black Robe had asked their father, the chieftain of the Quapaws, to let him pour the water of life on his daughter's head.

The chief had agreed, and the Black Robe had poured the water over the child's head and prayed to the Great Spirit. He had given her the name Mary, saying this was the name of the mother of the Man on the cross, and he had put the chain around her neck so that she would never forget.

His sister, Sun Eaglet said, had got well right away, but she could not remember any of this, for she was only three when it had happened. But after that her family had changed her name from Dawn Star to Star Mary. And since then she had worn the cross always. All this, the youth ended, had been many years ago. The Black Robe and the white man had stayed with the Quapaws only a few days and they had never seen them since.

Father Zenobius explained that the Black Robe was now in heaven with the Great Spirit. By questioning the children, he learned that they were indeed running away from the Chickasaws, and had to travel by night for fear of being caught. Now that they were close to the river, they were going to make a raft and pole their way across.

Father Zenobius tried to dissuade them from this and invited them to come instead with him. He would, he said, guide them to a great white chieftain who would gladly ransom them with fine gifts to the Chickasaws and take them home safely to their parents.

Great indeed was the joy of Sun Eaglet and Star Mary at this message. La Salle too was greatly pleased when they returned to the fort. It was a practice of his to request friendly tribes to sell him their war prisoners. In that way he was sure of a welcome when he returned the prisoners to their own people, a policy that enabled him to gain many friends among the tribes that lived along the Mississippi.

Despite the fortunate meeting with Sun Eaglet and Star Mary, however, the news that awaited Father Zenobius and Gabriel at the fort was disappointing. The search party had returned with the news that Pierre had not been found in the Chickasaw village.

Lieutenant Boisrondet shook his head glumly. "I don't know what the Commandant intends to do about searching further, but it's hardly possible Pierre can be alive after nine days."

A feeling of despair came over Gabriel. "Oh, Father, Father," he confided to the friar with a groan, "I'm sure the mitchybitchy must have killed him just as it would have killed us today."

Father Zenobius sighed. "I'm afraid it is so but you must not blame yourself. Promise me you will put that thought out of your mind."

"I'll try, Father," said the boy dully, and he turned away so that no one would see the tears in his eyes.

Somewhat apart from the rest he stood looking across the great river toward the setting sun—and seeing nothing. Suddenly his attention was caught by something spinning down the shore. It was a hollow tree, and in it was the figure of a man. He was bearded and his clothes were in rags; his hair was matted, his shrunken frame little better than a skeleton. But Gabriel's heart gave a great bound as recognition came, and a shout of joy burst from his throat.

"Look, it's Pierre—and he's alive!"

The weird figure waved a hand to them, then slumped down in the strange boat. Quickly a canoe was put out and Pierre was picked up. He was carried to the fort where Dr. Michel was waiting to attend him, and under his directions the starving man was fed and put to bed.

"He has been through a terrible experience but he's young and healthy and has a strong constitution," the doctor told La Salle. "After he is rested, he will soon recover. But I would not advise moving him for a week or more."

Next morning Pierre was able to tell them what had happened. "I was getting ready to make a fire and cook the little animal—what is it you call it?"

"An opossum," Lieutenant Boisrondet broke in.

"Enough," moaned the Breton feebly. "Never mention an opossum to me again, for it will always remind me of a worse American animal—the mitchybitchy."

Then he told them how the big cat, no doubt attracted by the scent of food, had leaped down before him and thrown him into such a panic that he had flung the carcass of the opossum at it and ran away without his gun.

At first he had been sure that he could find his way back to the fort, but this was the first time he had ever been alone in the wilderness. After a while he became hopelessly bewildered. The giant boughs of the huge trees shut out the sun and he lost all sense of direction. Instead of going south and west toward the camp on the bluffs, he traveled north, penetrating deeper and deeper into the swampy forest near the river.

Now and then a deer or bear started within a few yards of him but not one could he kill. He was starving in the midst of abundance. Sometimes he fed on weeds and grass and once he caught a turtle with his bare hands.

The nights were worse than the days, for the light of the moon and stars never penetrated into the forest. The darkness was intense except for the weird phosphorescent glow of the decayed tree trunks that lay around. The effect on one in his state of mind was uncanny, horrible.

Pierre told them that for several days he had heard no sound but the melancholy hooting of owls and the far-off bark of the fox. Only faith had kept him sane; he would lie down on the damp earth and pray. After a while he hardly knew what he was doing. Frantic from fatigue and hunger and anxiety, in the end he lost count of time.

At last he had found himself at the edge of the forest and had staggered out on a sandbar. There he found the hollow tree which some Indian had fashioned into a boat. Somehow he had managed to drag himself into it and shove off, letting the current carry him down the river. . . .

Now that Prudhomme had been rescued, the expedition could no longer delay in moving forward. Commandant La Salle left the invalid in the care of Sergeant Ayson, a veteran in his service and another expert woodsman, Andre Hunault. They had the aid of two of the Abenaki hunters; one of these was Running Elk, whose wife, a good nurse, also stayed behind.

"You'll be well taken care of here, Pierre," La Salle assured the Breton, "and we'll pick you up on the return voyage."

Tears of gratitude were falling down Pierre's wasted cheeks. He tried to rise from his sickbed. "You could have left me to die—"

La Salle checked him with a smile and grasped his hand. "Thank God, you are safe. Captain de Tonti and I have decided to dedicate this place to your rescue and call it Fort Prudhomme."

Pierre sank back. He found it hard to believe that after all the trouble he had caused, so great an honor could come to him.

Chapter 5

AMONG "THE BEAUTIFUL PEOPLE"

The explorers were long to remember the day they landed at the Quapaw village on the banks of the Arkansas River. Chief Sun, the father of the young hostages La Salle had bought from the Chickasaws, was the supreme ruler of all "the downstream folk"—the meaning of the word Arkansas. And royalty could not have received a more impressive welcome than the one he prepared for the Sieur de la Salle and his party.

The expedition had left the Chickasaw bluffs on March 6 and after a voyage of about 150 miles had come to the first village of the Quapaws on the west bank of the Mississippi. There Sun Eaglet and his sister Star Mary took one of the canoes of their own people and hurried on ahead to break the news to their father and give him time to prepare for the arrival of their rescuers.

Meantime Captain de Tonti ran into an unexpected piece of good luck: a young Illinois brave called Red Fox he had tried to help during an Iroquois raid on one of the Kaskaskia villages had found refuge among the friendly Quapaws. Here he had settled down quite contentedly, had taken a wife from their people, and learned their language.

Red Fox showed his joy at seeing "Iron Hand" and his comrades. He was more than willing to go down the river with them and act as their interpreter at the court of the great Chief Sun. He knew very little French, but De Tonti, like most of the white men who had lived among the Illinois, understood this Indian tongue and La Salle could speak it fluently. When they stopped at two more Quapaw villages on the Mississippi, they quickly saw how much help Red Fox could give them.

They reached the mouth of the Arkansas on the twelfth of March, the first moon of the Indian new year that began with spring. The day was beautiful, sunny and warm, the air soft and balmy, a day when anything pleasant and exciting, even amazing and wonderful, could happen.

The first surprise they met was the great flotilla that had gathered to meet them. Gabriel thought there must be at least 150 canoes and pirogues (dugouts made by hollowing out a tree trunk) bobbing there on the waters. And then he gulped in sheer astonishment, for coming along the bank to meet them was the most magnificent figure he had ever laid eyes on.

This man was very tall and very straight and wore a long robe of soft shining white cloth with a broad band around the hem embroidered in a red and gold design of rising suns. On his head was a crown with a red diadem embroidered in white kernel stones and snow-white swan's feathers, high in front and tapered down toward the back. The effect was sumptuous.

Gabriel was certain this could be no one less than the great Chief Sun himself come to welcome them in person. His ornaments alone were of regal splendor: bracelets and anklets of beaten copper, earrings of the finest slate beads Gabriel had ever seen and a wide neckplate of gleaming shells decorated with swastikas. Besides he had the grand

Chief Sun came to welcome them.

look of a born ruler with his fine features, high forehead and thin nostrils.

La Salle and the leaders of his party disembarked and went forward to meet Chief Sun. As they drew up before him the chief began to stroke La Salle's chest and made a strange clucking sound to show how glad he was to meet him. He did the same with Father Zenobius and Captain de Tonti, and then the members of his retinue followed his example all down the line. Before they knew it everyone was laughing and at ease.

"These are the friendliest Indians I have ever come across," the Commandant remarked in a low voice to De Tonti, as they were conducted back to their boats and guided up the river to the village a few leagues away. Here they were to meet more agreeable surprises.

They were led to a large square where a long table was set with an elaborate banquet that had been prepared by the women. It was a beautiful sight, for all around the square the peach trees were putting out their delicate pink blossoms. The chief sat at the head of the table on a throne—a carved divan with four feet; all cut from one piece of wood. Similar but smaller seats awaited his guests.

On his right hand Chief Sun placed Commandant de la Salle; on his left, De Tonti. Then came Father Zenobius and next to him Sun Eaglet. Gabriel's heart bounded happily when the Indian youth beckoned him to take the other place beside him.

Seated at the table with the white men were two heads of the different Quapaw clans—Gabriel learned later there were twenty-two—and the ranking warriors. Their own Indian escort sat around on the ground among the village folk, feasting on the lavish foods that were heaped before them.

Red Fox, in his role as interpreter, stood behind the great chief who had two servants to wait on him besides the large number that looked to the needs of the guests.

"The Sun King himself could boast no better service," Lieutenant de Boisrondet quipped, for it happened that this was one of the titles given to His Majesty Louis XIV of France.

"Speaking of royalty, my friend," said Captain d'Autray, "have you noticed the magnificence of the lady presiding at the other end of the table?"

Pearl Moon was even more handsomely bedecked than her husband. Her dress was of the same soft white silky material with the bodice made entirely of swan feathers. One shoulder was covered and the other left bare, and around her neck was a six-strand necklace of large, perfectly matched pearls. Long silver pendants dangled from her ears, and her arms both above and below the elbows were adorned with bracelets.

She was tall with a proud carriage and long, shining, black hair, cut short in front in a bang and fastened in a big bun at the back in a fine net. Two small silver fans held in place this elaborate headdress.

"Had she not quite so much red paint on her face, she could vie with the first beauties of the French Court," said the lieutenant. "As it is she might cause a little surprise—

"I find the pearls more fascinating than the lady," De Tonti murmured. "If they are real they are priceless. . . ."

The first course was sagamite, a favorite dish with the Indians, a gruel made from corn and given a rich flavor by mushrooms and the marrow bones of the buffalo. The pheasants that followed were the tenderest and juiciest the travelers had ever eaten; the turkey meat the most delicate;

there was no wild tang to the waterfowl. Nodding and beaming at their compliments, Chief Sun explained that all these various birds had been domesticated and fed by hand.

"Barnyard fowl among the Quapaws!" cried Martin de Launay. "Who would have dreamed of finding a race so civilized in the wilderness! And look at these fine spoons carved from buffalo horn," he went on. "And these dishes of all shapes and sizes!"

Commandant la Salle examined one of the red plates in open admiration. "This looks like excellent delftware," he exclaimed, "and what a beautiful color!"

"And the cloth from which the garments are made," De Tonti said. "We have seen nothing of this kind before in this part of the world."

"From what plant do you suppose the thread is made?" wondered Dr. Michel. "How do they prepare and weave it?"

"I'm told it is made from mulberry bark," said Father Zenobius. "Some of it is bleached and some of it is dyed like Chief Sun's red diadem and Star Mary's ribbons." As he spoke he smiled kindly at the little girl who was seated near her mother. She looked very pretty in her short yellow tunic embroidered in red swastikas and the bright ribbons in her dark glossy hair.

Gabriel wasn't paying too much attention to this talk. There was so much to eat, it was all so good, and between bites he was trying to talk to Sun Eaglet in the sign language. The chiefs son was eager to learn about guns which he called "the white men's lightning sticks."

Gabriel told him about his own firelock and why it had not gone off when he needed it so desperately. Sun Eaglet kept nodding his head to show that he understood. Gabriel could tell that even though the gun had failed to fire the Indian boy would gladly have traded his greatest treasures for such a weapon.

I ought to give him my gun, Gabriel thought to himself; he saved our lives. But he was almost sure the Commandant wouldn't like it if he did.

Sun Eaglet then spoke of his own fine bows and arrows. The bows were made of the hardest wood and would never wear out; the strings were thongs of hides. Gabriel asked him about the arrow he used when he killed the mitchy-bitchy, and Sun Eaglet explained it was the kind the hunters used against the buffalo. It was so deadly because it was tipped with the sharp scales of a mailed fish which the Indians fastened to the arrowhead with splits of cane and fish glue.

Now the servants were passing platters of tender broiled deer steaks served with cornbread baked on boards before the fire. Gabriel had never tasted such food—this and the sweet potatoes cooked in ashes and the beans boiled with savory herbs.

By the time the steaks were consumed, Gabriel was sure he couldn't swallow another morsel. Still there was one more course—little cakes made with honey and ground hickory nuts, morsels so tasty that he stowed away quite a few. So the meal went on and on until the guests had eaten and talked themselves into a pleasant drowsy state. The afternoon was nearly over before they rose from the table.

Gabriel's mouth was opening in a huge yawn when he noticed Captain de Tonti beckoning him. "Wake up, lad, I have a task for you."

Immediately Gabriel was wide awake. "Yes, sir," he said.

"Now listen carefully," went on De Tonti, handing Gabriel

a key. "Go to our baggage boat and unlock the big chest in which I keep my trading goods. You'll find a brass box with a colored picture painted on the cover. Bring this to me—and hurry."

Gabriel dashed away, always happy to obey the captain's orders. When he got back, De Tonti was waiting near a big log house that opened on the square. Red Fox, the interpreter, was with him.

"Good boy," said the captain as he pocketed the key. "We're going to pay a call on Chief Sun and his lady."

Chief Sun's house was the most beautiful Gabriel had ever been in. As the chief entered he invited his guests to sit on the low cane couches along the walls. They sank down on soft thick layers of bearskin; mats underneath covered the cane springs, and the doeskin pillows were stuffed with fragrant herbs.

A hole in the roof over the fireplace let the smoke out and admitted the light. In bad weather, Red Fox said, this was covered by a screen of stout hides mounted on a cane frame and fastened to the ceiling and operated with long hemp cords. The walls were hung with cane mats woven in different colors; spread out between them were gorgeous fans made of turkey feathers.

On a long shelf were displayed ornaments of intricate design: carved pipes; pottery bowls decorated with a bird's head and a frog; a little statue of a man kneeling and another of a seated woman. Wooden stands held articles that were both attractive and useful: a pitcher with a long spout that was cream colored outside and cherry red within; a pot decorated with circles of yellow and red. Wicker baskets with lids held the women's jewelry, trinkets and the vermilion for painting their faces.

The floor was covered with fine buffalo rugs, and in a corner stood a jug tall enough to hold forty pints of the bear oil the Indians rubbed on their skin. Although there was nothing more repellent to white men, Gabriel, of course, didn't mind. He'd used it himself until lately and knew there was nothing better to protect one's skin and keep the mosquitoes and other insects from biting.

As the visitors gazed around, their host was staring with lively interest at De Tonti's hand. It seemed he could hardly take his eyes from the strange-looking fist in the black glove.

Suddenly he reached out and grabbed De Tonti's hand in a gesture of friendship—and of curiosity. When he felt the hard metal hand, harder than anything he had ever touched, a squeal of surprise burst from him. He dropped the hand and fell back, a look of horror in his black eyes.

De Tonti turned to Red Fox. "Tell him about this hand," he said.

The Illinois bowed to him. "O mighty Iron Hand, I shall tell him."

Then turning to Chief Sun, Red Fox eloquently described how De Tonti had led the Illinois against their enemies, the Iroquois, and had won peace for his allies. Everywhere, the interpreter said, Chief Iron Hand was loved as well as feared, for though he was a dangerous foe he was a true friend. Of all the White Chiefs followers there was none who could compare with Iron Hand, none who understood the red man as he did.

Chief Sun looked and listened with growing attention. When Red Fox finished he placed his hands on De Tonti's chest and called him his "white brother." "Stay here with us, Chief Iron Hand," he added, "and I will give you land and slaves and anything you desire."

De Tonti could not have hoped for a better opening. He thanked Chief Sun for his great generosity but assured him he sought only his friendship. He said he had come to pay his respects to the chiefs consort and present her with a gift in token of his esteem.

Here he indicated the brass box that Gabriel was holding for him. The chief looked greatly pleased at this and sent for Pearl Moon to come at once.

For some reason that Gabriel couldn't understand, the captain was strangely excited. "Open up the box for me," he said, "and let's hope that she wears her pearls." And when the chief's wife walked in with the pearls around her neck Gabriel heard the captain softly exclaim: "By Jupiter, they *are* real! I must have them."

He gave her a sweeping bow and they all sat down. De Tonti then drew from the brass box a rope of large blue stones, the largest and prettiest beads Gabriel had ever seen. Pearl Moon clapped her hands like a child as De Tonti held the long necklace out to her and made signs for her to put it on. She slipped off her own necklace and began winding the blue beads around and around her neck.

Gabriel saw De Tonti's fingers closing over the pearl necklace. He was turning the pearls over in his hand, talking about them to the chief.

Gabriel didn't understand the language of the interpreter, so he could only guess at what was going on. The chief said something that pleased De Tonti very much, then he spoke to his wife. It was plain to see he was telling her to give Chief Iron Hand her pearl necklace.

Pearl Moon looked quite taken aback. She wanted the blue beads, of course, but she didn't want to part with her pearls. De Tonti pulled more jewels out of his treasure box—bracelets and anklets and earrings all made of the same lovely blue stones. He laid them before her; he invited her to try them on.

Gabriel blinked his eyes. What a dazzling sight! In his opinion if she turned them down she was just a poor savage without any sense.

Pearl Moon reached for a bracelet, then changed her mind. Now she was shaking her head. Alas, alas for his captain, she began unwinding the long ropes from her neck. Chief Sun seized her hand; he said something in a sharp voice. Pearl Moon hung her head and began to bite her lips.

De Tonti ran his hand through his hair, then flung himself on one knee before Pearl Moon. "Madame," he said, "the treasure chest is yours. Look inside and behold the most beautiful jewel of all."

Pearl Moon pushed back the lid and gave a little cry of wonder. She looked and looked—at herself! On the inside of the box was a mirror, the first she had ever seen.

She handed the box to her husband so he could look at himself too. Then they both began to laugh and laugh. Pearl Moon nodded her head; the pearls were handed to the captain.

"Thank God for the vanity of woman," said De Tonti once they were safely outside.

"I thought you got the worst of the bargain, sir," said Gabriel candidly.

De Tonti laughed gaily. "These pearls are real. The chief told me they found them in a river that empties into the Arkansas a short way from here. They call it the White River because its waters are so clear. Think of it, lad, a fortune in pearls for ten yards of glass!"

Gabriel had never seen Captain de Tonti so elated. He was grinning and whistling as they walked along. This was a side of his captain's nature the boy had never seen before, and he was still puzzled by the importance attached by so great a man to a mere string of beads.

The next day Gabriel broached this matter to Father Zenobius. "I don't understand why a string of pearls should mean so much to our captain," he said hesitantly.

"Oh, it was not for himself he wanted them," the friar explained, "but for our Commandant."

So that was it! All the time Captain de Tonti had wanted the pearls for someone else. Gabriel felt somehow happier now he had found this out. "But why," he insisted stubbornly, "are those pearls so important?"

"Gabriel, there are perhaps some things about this expedition that you do not understand. The Sieur de la Salle has dedicated his life to the great enterprise of discovery, but he has rivals and enemies among other groups of Frenchmen in Canada. They have representatives at the French Court as well as in the colonial government, and they've stopped at nothing to block and delay him—why, they've even accused him of misconduct!

"Of course there is no truth to these charges," Father Zenobius went on, "and until now the King has upheld the Sieur la Salle. But pressure is constantly brought to bear upon His Majesty to cede to others rights he has granted to our leader. Only recently the Commandant spoke of the necessity of finding some tangible evidence to prove to the King the value of his explorations and the riches of the land we are opening up. Now when the King sees the necklace, the perfection of the stones and the fine workmanship of the Indians, he is bound to be impressed."

Gabriel nodded. "Thank you, Father. Now I understand. Those pearls will make the finest of gifts for King Louis."

On the second day of their stay among the Quapaws on the banks of the Arkansas, La Salle and his companions were entertained by the Dance of the Calumet. The happiness of peace was its theme, symbolized by the calumet or peace pipe.

Forty youths, bare to the waist, and with feathered headdress, formed a long procession with Sun Eaglet at their head. During the elaborate pantomime that followed, the leader held aloft a large pipe with a stem of polished red stone, its bowl decorated with eagle feathers. At the same time the Indian maidens sang and performed to music a graceful dance showing the joys of peace and good will.

Next came the exchange of gifts. The Indians were made very happy, for La Salle and his aides had made ample provision for all. To the men they gave knives and hatchets, axes and mattocks. The women marveled over iron pots and kettles, scissors and needles. Finally the visitors distributed combs and bells and many other trinkets to delight the Indians of all ages.

La Salle then arose to make the presentation, an imposing figure in his military uniform with scarlet coat braided in gold and the gold epaulets on his shoulders. The Quapaws could not take their eyes from him. They were fascinated by his words as well as by his commanding presence and by the eloquence of his gestures as he told them about the Great White Father far across the ocean. These gifts, he said, were really from His Majesty King Louis XIV of France and were the sign of his regard for them. To all who dwelt under his banner he was a good and loving father, a strong protector against their enemies and a faithful guardian of their rights.

All this the Commandant told them. Then he spoke of his own plans, and how he hoped that this was just the beginning of a lasting alliance that would bring wonderful benefits both to Frenchmen and to the Quapaw nation.

The Quapaws, not to be outdone in generosity, now loaded their friends with presents—their choicest pelts and a large supply of provisions for the journey. Above all the explorers welcomed the large amount of parched meal made of beans and cornmeal, exceptionally nourishing and the best of all staples for a long journey.

Chief Sun gave La Salle special gifts to take back to France to present to King Louis. One of the gifts was the white cloth of the Indians made from the bark of the mulberry tree. Others were samples of their healing herbs and medicines: the rattlesnake herb which, when the root was chewed and also applied to the wound for five or six hours, extracted the poison of the venomous reptile; the inner bark of the "toothache tree" that needed only to be rolled up to the size of a pea and laid on the aching tooth until pain ceased; and a balm from the sweet gum tree to reduce fever and cure many other ills.

After these ceremonies Father Zenobius went among the people, trying to tell them of the Great Spirit who was their loving Father in heaven. He taught them the Lord's Prayer and a few basic truths of the Christian Faith.

They flocked around him, drawn by his winning, amiable ways and the tidings of the gospel he brought them. As for Father Zenobius he would have asked for nothing better than to remain among these amiable, hospitable people, so open, it seemed, to the Christian message. "Days in an earthly paradise among the Beautiful People" was the way he was to record this sojourn among the Quapaws.

The evening of the second day was spent by La Salle and

Captain de Tonti in deep conference with Chief Sun and the head men of the nation. At that meeting Chief Sun graciously consented to place his people and the country of the Arkansas under the protection of the King of France. He also agreed to allow Father Zenobius to plant the cross of Christ among them as a sign of approval.

When these measures were announced next day the friar was overcome with joy and started at once to direct the building of the cross. He chose the wood of the ash tree; though very strong and durable it was light and easy to hew down and split. The cross was finished very quickly, for many willing hands—Gabriel's among them—went into its making.

With his own hands Father Zenobius planted the cross in the ground. How tall and fair and straight it stood in the bright sunlight! Then the Commandant fastened to it the fleur-de-lis of France and the seal of His Most Christian Majesty, Louis XIV. In the King's name he took possession of this country and nation located on the west bank of the Mississippi near the mouth of the River Arkansas.

But the ceremony was not over. Again La Salle motioned for attention. He was smiling as he dropped a hand on Captain de Tonti's shoulder and said in a loud voice: "By the right and privilege granted to me by the King of France to form habitations on the lands in the territory of which I have taken possession in the King's name, I do hereby grant Chevalier Henri de Tonti, my faithful aide and trusted friend, the right to build a settlement in this province on the Arkansas River."

For a moment there was silence, for this was an utter surprise—even to Captain de Tonti. All the members of the expedition applauded loudly and crowded about him to congratulate him. As soon as the Quapaws understood, they shared in the jubilation. Especially was Chief Sun happy, for it meant that Iron Hand would return to them.

Then it was that four of the Indians and their families who had accompanied the explorers from Fort St. Joseph expressed their wish to remain among the Quapaws. To this Captain de Tonti readily assented, for it fitted in very well with his plans. They could, he said, await his own return to the banks of the Arkansas.

As De Tonti spoke Sun Eaglet looked earnestly at Gabriel. "Promise you will come back with him," he entreated. "There is an old saying that he who drinks the waters of the Arkansas will never be satisfied anywhere else."

"I promise," Gabriel assured him. He was quite certain that wherever Captain de Tonti went, there he would go also.

La Salle granted De Tonti land rights in Arkasas.

Chapter 6

THE GREAT DISCOVERY

Once more the expedition moved down the great winding river. Chief Sun had provided his friends with two guides to take them to the chief of the Taensas, the next nation to the south. These Indians lived on a lake several leagues inland from the Mississippi, and the only way to reach their village was on foot through swampy woods. One of the guides chosen by Chief Sun was Red Fox who could continue to act as interpreter. He and his companion were instructed to see to it that the white strangers were cordially received by the Taensas who were the Quapaws' allies.

Paddling downstream La Salle and his voyagers passed two more Quapaw villages—passed without stopping. A long journey lay before them and pauses were made only when it became absolutely necessary to hunt for fresh provisions. It was March 22 when they reached the point on the river nearest the Taensas village.

Captain de Tonti and the Indian guides disembarked and immediately started inland to inform the Taensas of La Salle's arrival. Their chief received De Tonti with a smiling face and invited him to his dwelling—a large hut forty feet square made of mud and covered with cane mats.

In some ways De Tonti found the Taensas even more civilized than the Quapaws. There was, for instance, a handsome temple to the sun god adorned with sculptures of three eagles. But this temple was surrounded by a spiked wall on which were impaled the withered heads of enemies sacrificed to the god. De Tonti also learned that the Taensas practiced polygamy—unknown among the Quapaws—and when their ruler died his youngest wife, his house steward and a hundred men were sacrificed and buried with him.

Nevertheless De Tonti found the Taensas as friendly and amiable to white men as were the Quapaws, their country rich and fertile. As the chief readily agreed to come to confer with La Salle the following day, De Tonti and his guides returned at once to tell the Commandant of the approaching visit. That night the voyagers camped on an island in the river.

Next morning they heard the sound of drums and the voices of women singing. When the Taensas' canoes reached the island, La Salle paid royal honors to the ruler who came attended by several of his courtiers, old men dressed like himself in long white robes made from the bark of the mulberry tree. The Indians brought gifts—a large and welcome store of provisions and lengths of their white cloth. In return La Salle gave them presents, and after smoking the calumet of peace they departed well satisfied.

After the Taensas had gone, Red Fox and his companion came to bid farewell to Chief Iron Hand. Their mission had been accomplished and they were returning to their Quapaw village.

"Tell the great Chief Sun of our gratitude for all he has done, and of the kindness shown us by his Taensas allies," said De Tonti. As they left he paused regretfully to watch these good friends start back on their difficult passage up the river, paddling against the current.

The southward voyage was resumed and almost immediately the explorers began to see and kill alligators, hideous creatures with bodies fifteen to twenty feet long. Their legs were so short they were helpless on land, but menacing and dangerous in the water.

The following day a canoe was sighted and the Commandant ordered his men to follow it. De Tonti's boat set out and was just on the point of overtaking it when more than a hundred Indians appeared on the east bank of the river.

"Come back," shouted La Salle. "Come back."

The captain obeyed promptly and rejoined the others, after which they camped opposite the natives on the west bank.

"I wish we could meet them peaceably," said La Salle.

That was enough for De Tonti. He set out in his canoe at once and went to meet the Indians, holding aloft the calumet. On seeing this, the natives joined their hands as a sign that they wished to be friends.

"Join your hands together as they do," De Tonti ordered those with him in the canoe. "I have but one hand and cannot."

No one could be more persuasive than the captain when he wanted. Very shortly the chief men among the Indians were crossing the river with him to meet La Salle. The latter received them with overtures of peace and friendship, smoked the peace pipe with them and gave them presents.

So cordial were the relations on both sides that La Salle and some of his men went with these Indians to their village where the Commandant passed the night with their chief. He learned that they were a tribe of Natchez and that the chief's brother was the ruler of the nation, a strong one with more than three hundred warriors. His village was situated on a hillside near the river eighteen miles farther south on this same eastern shore.

"Will you take me to him?" La Salle asked. The chief agreed, and with a party of his warriors accompanied the white men down the river. Under such escort they were almost sure of a friendly reception, nor were they disappointed. The head of the Natchez nation showed toward them the same affable disposition as had the other Mississippi River folk they had met.

Their manner and customs were similar too. The Natchez villages were built around large public squares; they held assemblies; engaged in sports and games; were lively and active. They lived in permanent dwellings, hunted, fished and cultivated the soil, for nature was as generous here as she was in all the other fruitful regions bordering on this vast and wonderful inland sea. More presents were given and taken, an alliance cemented.

Once again the canoes started downstream. On and on for sixty miles they journeyed when a great river came rushing from the west—a river with waters as red as blood. At first the voyagers were startled, not knowing the cause of the strange phenomenon. It was soon explained, for the river banks were formed of the reddest clay they had ever seen, and when washed down it turned the water to scarlet. That was why it was called the Red River.

That night they camped near the mouth of this waterway and in the morning their canoes crossed a great canal. Could this mean they had almost reached the ocean? Perhaps it lay just around the next sharp bend? Hope quickened their pace but each new turn brought only more islands, more peninsulas, more crescents of shifting sands. For mile after mile it was the same shoreline of swamps and canebrakes and shoals of alligators.

After ninety miles they saw on the right a wide sandbank where men were fishing. Here La Salle was forced to order a halt, for his men had run short of food and had had nothing to eat for several days but potatoes. He made the usual overtures and offered gifts to these Indians who were known as the Quinipassas. They took the white men's presents and gave them food, inviting them to stay the night.

The Quinipassas behaved most treacherously, for at dawn they attacked the sleeping visitors. Fortunately De Tonti awakened immediately and quickly aroused his men. A fierce battle followed in which the Quinipassas were soundly trounced and their canoes burned. These were the only hostile Indians met on the entire voyage, and henceforth they were to remember and respect the might of Chief Iron Hand.

After this experience the voyagers at once tried to put as much distance as possible between themselves and the unfriendly natives. The Mississippi was now at its broadest, fully four miles wide. The sun was still high in the sky and the weather fine, one of those early spring days with a fresh wind blowing and just warm enough to be pleasant.

That day they made good time, covering more than thirty miles. Then off in the distance beyond the timber-line they were startled to see flocks of buzzards and carrion crows wheeling slowly above a hillside. Before they reached the place where the vultures hovered, a dreadful stench assailed their nostrils. Then the scene in all its sickening horror came into view. A whole village—they learned later it belonged to the Tangibaos Indians—had been totally destroyed by some savage enemy. The remains of the dead were everywhere, some piled in heaps as if intended for a bonfire. All the cabins were burned to the ground; only a few charred walls had been left standing.

Gabriel could scarcely breathe. In a flash he lived again that awful time long ago when the Iroquois had slain his parents. This was more than he could bear, and he turned away, shaken and heartsick, wishing he had never come ashore.

The others were moved too. They were fighting men, hardened to violence and death, but all of them would have blotted out this ghastly sight if it had been possible.

"It must have happened about eight days ago," Gabriel heard De Tonti say to the Commandant.

A shadow lowered over La Salle's face. He shivered. "To die like this is a grievous thing, but to lie unburied and become the prey of the wolves and the vultures"— his voice caught and added—"what fate could be more horrible?"

It was good to get away, to shove off on the big water and fill one's lungs with the pure, untainted air.

On the seventh day of April, after covering 120 more miles, the explorers at last floated within sight of the Gulf. The approach was frightful to the eye, for the whole immense vista was a seething quagmire through which the river cut its way in three channels to the sea. All the sand and ooze, all the uprooted trees and canes and debris swept along by the mighty stream and poured into it by its great tributaries were piled up here. This was the delta, a monstrous plain of mud that thrust into the Gulf like the webbed foot of some titanic goose.

But the purpose of the expedition had not yet been fully accomplished. It was of the utmost importance to discover where the channels emptied and whether they were navigable. So La Salle divided his men into three parties, one to inspect each channel. He took the middle one himself, De Tonti the right and D'Autray the left.

Six miles down the channel La Salle and his party found salt water and the deep blue waves of the Gulf of Mexico lapped at their feet. It was late the next day when the other two groups returned and they all had the same report to make—the channels were very fine, wide and deep.

Now La Salle knew beyond doubt that large ships could sail down the Mississippi to the sea, and what was more that ships from the ocean could enter the river and travel up it. This meant that his dream of years could be realized, that all the inland parts of the huge continent of North America could be linked in a vast system of transportation. It meant the opening up of many settlements, the cultivation of great tracts of fertile lands, trade with the natives and commerce with Europe.

That night the happy voyagers made camp above the marshes on a neck of firm land on the right bank. This narrow strip with its fringe of cottonwoods and a few other trees well suited the Commandant's intention. He had one more thing to do before the celebration of their victory: he must build a cross. He said now, as he had said before: "His Majesty would annex no country to his crown without implanting therein the Christian religion."

La Salle named the country "Louisiana"

The cross was planted deep on this high dry spot overlooking the sea. And at its foot was buried a copper plate with the Latin inscription: "Louis the Great, King of France reigns; this the ninth day of April, 1682." To make doubly sure of the claim, La Salle fastened the King's coat of arms, bearing the same inscription, to a nearby tree.

The moment had now arrived for which they had journeyed twelve hundred miles down the Mississippi from the mouth of the Illinois to the Gulf of Mexico.

Two by two the procession formed. At its head was La Salle with Father Zenobius at his side; next came Captains de Tonti and d'Autray, and behind them in the order of their rank the rest of the company.

They were silent as they looked upon their leader and awe filled many hearts as the simple but formal ceremony began. La Salle's voice was strong and clear as in the name of Louis XIV and his successors to the crown of France he took possession "of the Mississippi, of all rivers that entered it, and all the country watered by them." And he named this inland empire "Louisiana" in honor of his King.

Now remained only the witnessing of the *procès verbal* or document of La Salle's discovery. The notary, Jacques de la Metairie, had prepared the official report of their voyage and all the Frenchmen signed. The first after the Sieur de la Salle to affix his signature was Captain Henri de Tonti.

Now salvos were fired in salute to the King, and as Father Zenobius gave his blessing all voices were raised in the glorious hymn of the *Te Deum*.

Chapter 7

A Fruitless Search

Four years were to pass before De Tonti kept his promise to return to the Quapaws. Quite without warning, on a blustery March day in 1686, Chief Iron Hand came paddling up the Arkansas. He rode at the head of a line of canoes bearing twenty-five Frenchmen and five Illinois and Shawnee Indians. Next to him sat Lieutenant Gabriel La Grue, a boy no longer. At twenty he had earned his commission in hard-fought campaigns against the Iroquois while stationed with De Tonti, now commandant of Fort St. Louis on the Illinois River.

The Quapaws gave De Tonti and his companions a royal welcome. First to greet them was the son of the chief, now fully grown and entitled to wear the eagle-feather headgear of a proud warrior. His name had been changed to Sun Eagle as befitted a man of twenty-one. With him came Star Mary, no longer a pretty child but a maiden of sixteen and lovely as a flower.

Chief Sun and his wife Pearl Moon soon put in their appearance. Overjoyed, they took it for granted that Chief Iron Hand had returned to stay among them, and Chief Sun wanted to start at once a three days' celebration of feasting and dancing and games.

A cloud came over Captain de Tonti's face as he told them this was impossible and tried to explain to them the sad reason for this visit. How much had happened since their happy meeting in 1682!

After the discovery of the mouth of the Mississippi he and La Salle had started on a hurried journey back to Quebec to report their findings to the officials of New France. The Commandant had fallen sick and his aide had gone forward alone to present the report. But the captain had not long lingered in Quebec, for news had reached him that the Iroquois were again on the warpath against the Illinois villages and that his presence in the troubled area was sorely needed.

At La Salle's command he had begun at once to build a new fort on the Illinois River since it had become necessary to abandon Fort Crevecoeur farther to the south. The new garrison was called St. Louis and stood on a solid rock six hundred feet in circumference and towering 125 feet above the water. Under its protection the scattered Illinois had returned to their villages and other friendly tribes had settled nearby. After his recovery La Salle had joined De Tonti and both were engaged in their work among the Indians when in 1683 news reached them that the new governor of Canada— spurred on by La Salle's enemies among the merchants—had deprived him of all his authority, confiscated his estates, and was about to seize the forts he had built.

Accompanied by Father Zenobius, La Salle had immediately set out for France to obtain justice or at least a hearing. The news of his discovery had gone well before him and he was received by King Louis with every mark of approval and affection. He was vindicated against his enemies, his rights were restored, and new favors were granted him. The King made him governor of the territory he had just discovered and heartily approved of his new plan to sail from France direct to the Gulf of Mexico with the necessary men and supplies to start a colony at the mouth of the Mississippi.

Up until this time La Salle had paid all the expenses of his expeditions. Now the King placed a man-of-war, the *Joly,* at his disposal and gave him outright a small frigate, the *Belle.* One hundred soldiers were detailed to him and he was given ten thousand livres to pay their wages for a year. He was also authorized to levy a hundred more men at his own expense.

Since the colony was to be a permanent one, La Salle provided all that would be required, chartering two more vessels to carry everything. The *Amiable,* a ship of three hundred tons, was loaded with food and supplies and even material to build a blacksmith shop and two chapels. A ketch or small-decked craft, the *St. François,* carried thirty tons of ammunition, including cannon for the fort La Salle intended to build for safeguarding his settlement.

Six priests accompanied the expedition to care for the spiritual needs of the colonists and to convert the Indians. Three, including La Salle's brother the Abbé, then back in France, were Sulpicians. Father Zenobius was returning with two more Recollect Fathers.

Altogether there were 280 people aboard the four boats when the squadron set sail on July 24, 1864 from La Rochelle.

The King's men accounted for a hundred, the ships' officers and crews for around seventy, and the rest were La Salle's own recruits: craftsmen and workers of all sorts, and a group of citizens of Rouen who were interested in the new venture.

One was a young nobleman, the Marquis de la Sablonière, another a surgeon, Liotot, and two brothers Duhaut who had sunk considerable money in the enterprise. Then there was Sergeant Henri Joutel who had served seventeen years in the army.

La Salle also took along two young nephews, Crevel de Moranget, about eighteen, and Nicolas Cavelier, who was only a small boy. However, there were women aboard to keep an eye on him. Two were widows, one with several children of her own; the other six were young women who hoped to marry and settle down in the new land.

All these things De Tonti had learned in letters and messages sent to him by his Commandant before the expedition had set sail from France. He had been well pleased with the news for it fitted in perfectly with his plan for his own settlement among the Quapaws. The Arkansas post would make an excellent trading center between the upper and the lower Mississippi.

Knowing the hazards and delays of travel, De Tonti had waited patiently for over a year to hear of the arrival on the Gulf of La Salle's expedition. He had allowed for the slow passage of boats across the Atlantic and for the time for news to reach him by a courier traveling from the lower reaches of the Mississippi to his station at Fort Louis on the Illinois. But when yet another eight months had passed and no word had come, De Tonti was seriously concerned. He finally decided to undertake again the long voyage down the Mississippi to look for La Salle and his colonists.

"So, happy as we are to be back among you, my friends," De Tonti said to Chief Sun and his Quapaws, "you will understand from what I have said that we cannot linger, and that all other plans must wait until we have found our Commandant."

Chief Sun nodded. "All we ask is that you bring us good news of your lost chieftain."

So De Tonti's search party took leave and hurried onward down the river. Among their number were other members of the first expedition, including, besides Gabriel La Grue, Jean Couture and Martin de Launay.

Hope rode with them as the canoes spun down the swift-flowing current. On this second voyage they could travel much faster, for they did not have to pause to make friends. Wherever they stopped red men urged them to stay, but in each place they delayed only long enough to exchange greetings and stock provisions.

They recognized sights they had seen on their first voyage: deep bends in the river; islands where they had slept under the stars; the crimson waters of the Red River and the great canal below it. Then the dwindling forests, the reeds and great muddy plains of the delta.

It was April 10 and Holy Week had begun. A little more than four years to the day had passed since they had caught their first glance of the Gulf. But forgotten now was the glory of that moment, the wild exultant thrill. In all the lonely waste of mud and water no sign of La Salle's great enterprise was to be found. Only lying there, half buried in the slime where the floods had thrown it down, was the cross he had raised.

Was this the answer, this fallen cross, the copper plate buried in the mud? What evil omen was here? Could this have been the end of La Salle's quest?

Uneasy looks betrayed the grim forebodings of their hearts, but Henri de Tonti was not the man to weaken in the face of disaster. "Men," he said to his little band, "they must have missed the mouth of the river. It isn't hard to see how that could happen to a ship searching for it along the coast."

Couture looked at their leader. "That's right," he nodded. "The Spanish used to call it Rio Escondido, the Hid River."

"And no wonder," answered De Tonti. "Do you remember how the delta sands curve around in the shape of a crescent so that they almost hide the river's mouth? It would be hard enough, as all of you know, to find the channels from the sea even in fair weather. If the Commandant's ships ran into a storm or fog, they'd never have seen them."

"Could they have been lost at sea even before reaching the Gulf?" asked Gabriel, his anxiety written over his face.

De Tonti shook his head. "I'm sure not," he said confidently. "They must have landed elsewhere along the coast. What we'll have to do is to divide into groups. One party can search east toward Florida, while the rest of us explore the coast toward Mexico. We'll take canoes and start early in the morning. Perhaps before the day is out, one or other of us will find the colonists."

The search parties made camp on the spot where La Salle had erected the cross. For seven days they searched east and west along the Gulf coast. At last when they ran out of water and were forced to return to camp, the men gave up hope. It was useless to search further. Even De Tonti admitted that the colonists who had set out so bravely from France must have met with disaster.

It was a sad and silent group of men who, on Easter Monday, began the return journey upstream. When they had paddled about fifteen miles up the river, Captain de Tonti gave the order to halt. He himself built a new standard to replace the fallen cross, and planted it firmly in high ground where the Mississippi floods could not touch it. Then he placed a silver écu, a large coin stamped with the King's image, in the hollow of a tree to mark the place and the date.

De Tonti placed a silver coin in the hollow of the tree.

Once again the party shoved off into the current, rowing hard against it as they made their way toward the Arkansas. When they came opposite the village of the treacherous Quinipassas, to their astonishment they were met by the chiefs with the calumet and signs of good will.

This time De Tonti was willing to make an alliance with this tribe; it fitted in with his plans. Somewhere in the wilderness to the west, he was sure that his lost leader was trying to find his way back to the Mississippi. Perhaps he was struggling through the mesquite bushes of an arid desert or wading through swampy wastelands. Perhaps at this moment the Commandant was not far away.

So he wrote a letter to La Salle and gave it to the Quinipassas to guard carefully in case he should come. The Indians stared in wonder at "the talking leaves" covered with the bold flourishes of his quill. Though he had had to learn to write anew with his left hand, De Tonti's penmanship was amazingly fine.

"Sir," he wrote, "having found the column on which you placed the arms of France thrown down, I caused a new one to be erected, about seven leagues from the sea. All the nations have sung the calumet. These people fear us extremely since our attack upon their village. I close by saying that it gives me great uneasiness to be obliged to return under the misfortune of not having found you. Two canoes have examined the coast thirty leagues toward Mexico and twenty-five toward Florida."

The letter was dated April 20, 1686.

Some weeks later the search party was back among the Quapaws and there De Tonti made one last effort. He called for volunteers to stay in the Arkansas country and watch and wait for La Salle.

"Perhaps even now he's searching for the Arkansas River," he said. "He knows that when he reaches it, he'll be safe. I want him to find some of us waiting for him. I want a house where he can rest and be taken care of."

"I'll stay, sir," Gabriel assured him, "if you wish it."

De Tonti looked pleased. "I do, Lieutenant. This will give pleasure to your friend Sun Eagle and it will give you a chance to learn the Quapaw language."

Couture and De Launay were also eager to stay. Aside from their concern for La Salle—and they'd admired him from the time they were boys in Normandy—they were well satisfied to linger in so ideal a spot.

"If you are to build you'll need some workers and someone to operate a forge," went on De Tonti. "Three will be enough."

Michaud and La Violette, skilled carpenters, agreed to stay and La Forge, the blacksmith, was also willing.

Now that this was settled, De Tonti had another long journey before him. He must go to Quebec to make a report of his fruitless search to Governor de Denonville. Then he must return to his Fort St. Louis command. It was dangerous to be away too long from the 20,000 Indian allies who were living there under his protection.

"It will be October before I get back from Quebec," he told the little band he was leaving. "But if you have any news send it to me immediately, either there or at Fort St. Louis." And he ended gravely, "Meantime, wait and watch."

Captain de Tonti's house was built on the north bank of the Arkansas across the river from the Quapaw village, on a high spot beyond the reach of floods. The place was near enough to the Indian village to see the tall cross Father Zenobius had planted in the square those years before. The

Quapaws had surrounded it with a neat palisade of strong cane to keep it safe until the priest returned to them.

The Indians helped their white friends clear the land and hew the cypress logs for the dwelling. "Chief Iron Hand's house will last forever," they said, for cypress never rots in air or water. They came from miles about to see the wonderful house built by the Frenchmen, with its door and windows and a floor of stout puncheon slabs. No less of a marvel to them was the clay chimney that carried off the smoke of the fireplace.

When it was all finished, the simple furniture made and the big iron pots hung over the hearthstone, De Tonti's men were proud of their handiwork. "The first building of its kind west of the Mississippi," Couture gloated.

His friend Martin de Launay agreed. "Imagine how it will look to Commandant la Salle and his lost wanderers!"

Gabriel was silent, wondering when they would see the Commandant again. There was something relentless in the sure, steady passage of the days, the weeks. Then he reminded himself sternly of De Tonti's charge: "Watch and wait."

Meantime there was much to be done. They cleared more land and planted it; hunted the wild herds, skinned and dressed the hides, prepared and dried the meat; they fished and swam in the river. Scarcely a day passed that they did not visit their friends in the village or see Sun Eagle's canoe paddling across the stream.

The rich soil yielded an abundant harvest. The maize was ground, the fruits dried, the vegetables stored. Autumn was at hand and the two carpenters and the blacksmith decided to go back to the Illinois country. Their work on Captain de Tonti's house was finished and they wished to return to him.

Lieutenant Couture gave them a routine report to carry.

"And tell him we'll stay until we have news of the Commandant," he ended. "He can count on us."

"When you tell the captain how things are prospering here at his post on the Arkansas," De Launay added, "be sure to add that I for one would gladly stay for the rest of my life."

Gabriel was the last to clasp their hands in farewell. "Tell the captain I can speak Quapaw fairly well. And be sure to give my regards to Pierre and Sergeant Ako and the Picard." Those old friends were comfortably settled on land grants around Fort St. Louis, and Prudhomme was now the official gunsmith for the garrison.

The young men watched the long canoe until it turned a bend in the Mississippi, then they paddled back up the Arkansas. The autumn tints of the trees reflected in the limpid waters were so beautiful and life could be so carefree in this land of sunshine, easy laughter and amiable ways. If only, Gabriel thought, the heavy clouds of anxiety would lift, if suddenly the tall commanding figure of the Sieur de la Salle would step forth from the dark forest. When, oh when, would that day come?

Chapter 8

A Tale of Treachery

Ten more months went by before news of any kind reached De Tonti's post on the banks of the Arkansas. On July 20, 1687, a party of Quapaws were out cutting trees in a nearby wood when they saw seven wraiths—six bearded men and a boy—stumbling toward them. The Indians at once led these piteous refugees to their village.

A wild surge of joy swept over Gabriel La Grue when, as he stood before De Tonti's house, he first caught sight of the ragged figures. Across the water he could see that one wore a gray robe and another looked like Commandant la Salle. He picked up his gun and fired three salvos, then leaped into a canoe while Couture and De Launay ran to man a second boat. As they paddled madly across the river toward the

village, they saw the travelers fall down on their knees before the cross.

"Look," Couture shouted a few moments later, "they're coming down the bank."

"They see us," De Launay cried out. "They see the house."

As their canoes reached midstream Gabriel became dreadfully cast down. The friar in the tattered gray robe was a stranger and the tall man with straggling gray hair was not La Salle although his shriveled masklike face somewhat resembled him.

"It's the Commandant's brother, the Abbé Cavelier," he heard Couture saying.

ie ragged travelers fell on their knees before the cross.

"And the big fellow with the black spade beard is Henri Joutel," De Launay said. "I've never seen any of the others."

"The boy must be the Commandant's nephew," Gabriel reasoned. "But where—" He couldn't finish and a chill struck to every heart.

Later—after the survivors were carried to the log house and given food and drink—De Tonti's aides learned the shocking fate of their lost leader and his companions.

As De Tonti had suspected, the ships had missed the mouth of the river and had gone far west. Ill luck and trouble had pursued them from the start. The Spaniards appeared suddenly and seized the ketch loaded with cannon and ammunition, and there was constant friction between La Salle and Captain de Beaujeau, his naval commander.

Sergeant Joutel, who was giving this account, accused De Beaujeau of the blackest treachery. "Oh, that wicked man!" he said. "He deliberately wrecked the *Amiable*, stranded and grounded her on the shoals during the night. One of the blackest, most detestable actions! Then our frigate, the *Belle*, was maliciously staved in, also in the night.

"Soon thereafter a number of the colonists wanted to go back to France, and Beaujeau set sail with them in the *Joly*. Such blows of fortune! Our Commandant had need of all his resolution to bear up against them, but his courage did not forsake him. He made a temporary fort out of the wrecked *Amiable* and put me in command. Then he set out along the coast with five canoes carrying fifty men.

"They did not find an arm of the Mississippi as the Commandant had hoped they would, but on a bay the Spaniards call Matagorda, they came across a good site for our settlement. There with great toil and hardship they built a fort. More than thirty of the men died. They even lost the master carpenter, and what a misfortune that was."

"But the Commandant," interrupted Couture, "did he give up the idea of finding the mouth of the Mississippi?"

"Never!" answered Joutel firmly. "Once the fort was built and the remaining colonists had been settled there, the Commandant made two long journeys in search of the river. The first was started in October, 1685. He put me in charge of the fort and took twenty men with him, including the younger Duhaut. Months passed and we heard nothing from him. The men at the fort began to mutter. The elder Duhaut began to stir up trouble and he had little difficulty doing it with men who were ripe for rebellion and mutiny."

"Was there nothing you could do to stop Duhaut?" Couture's voice was filled with amazement.

Sergeant Joutel groaned and struck his head in bitter remorse. "If only I had put him in irons then for the scheming traitor he was! Instead I gave him a severe reprimand and threatened him with prison if I caught him stirring up the men again. The others I tried to encourage with hopeful words.

"But then when Commandant la Salle came back in August, things grew worse. In the first place he had failed again, and then only eight men of the twenty who had started out were still with him. Four had taken to the woods—simply deserted and gone to live with the Indians.

"But what really brought the rebellion to a head was the news that the Commandant had given five of the men leave to turn back because they were unable to endure the fatigue of the journey. Since they hadn't found their way back to the fort, it was certain they had fallen into the hands of the savages and had been killed. And among them was the younger Duhaut.

"It was terrible to see the rage and grief of the elder Duhaut. He swore a solemn oath never to forgive the Sieur de la Salle and to avenge the death of his brother. Nothing that we could say would persuade him that it was not the fault of the Commandant."

"But that is so unreasonable!" De Launay exploded.

"Unreasonable?" Joutel shrugged. "Of course it was unreasonable. But the Commandant kept his temper, and soon he was able to raise everyone's hopes. He began to make new plans—this time he would travel overland to the north to the country of the Quapaws. Once safely with them he would go on upriver to join Captain de Tonti at the fort on the Illinois. He spoke constantly of his desire to see the captain and of the need for his assistance."

Joutel was silent for a moment, and his hearers moved restlessly waiting for him to go on with his account.

"In January of this year," the sergeant resumed slowly, "we started on the fatal journey. We left Father Zenobius with the colonists at the fort; he wept when we said good-by and told the Commandant he had never before felt such sorrow at a parting.

"Of those who started out that day there were the seven you see whom God in his compassion has guided safely here. Then there was the Commandant's older nephew, young Moranget, and our leader's servants, a Frenchman named Saget, and Nica, his faithful Shawnee. Besides there were the untrustworthy ones: Liotot the surgeon, Duhaut and his creature L'Archeveque and the German pirate Heins to whom our Commandant had taken an odd liking.

"Duhaut and Liotot were burning with resentment and they had their following. More than two weary, hopeless years had passed since we had begun the search for the Mississippi.

They had invested their money in the Commandant's grand plan and got nothing but bitter disappointment, hard luck and grief. All the time their hatred was building up against our commander. It was ready to explode, and in a little more than two months it did.

"A trivial matter unloosed their fury. Provisions were running low and Duhaut and Liotot went out on a scouting party with Nica and others. The Shawnee killed two bullocks and they sent Saget back to camp with the good news. Young Moranget and the servant returned with a pack horse and instructions from Commandant de la Salle to bring back a load immediately, leaving the rest of the meat to be dried. When Moranget arrived and saw the others had smoked both beeves without waiting for them to dry, and found them sitting before a huge fire feasting on choice parts of the meat, he flew into a childish rage and screamed out abuses.

"It was like lighting a fuse to a keg of dynamite. Then and there Duhaut and his accomplices resolved on a bloody revenge on one they now regarded as their most hated enemy. They would murder the nephew, and they would also have to kill the servant and Nica because they were so loyal to our leader.

"So they waited until the three had eaten their supper and had fallen asleep. The surgeon was the inhuman executioner. He took an axe and struck Moranget over and over on the head, then did the same to the Indian and Saget.

"This slaughter satisfied only a part of the revenge of these murderers. They must now destroy the main object of their hatred. But the river was too swollen for them to return to camp, and so it came about that the Commandant himself walked, all unsuspecting, into their trap."

Suddenly the big, bearded man seemed on the verge of

collapse. He turned to the silent friar. "Father Anastasius, you were there," he said shakily. "You tell them—"

So, with a sigh, the young Recollect finished the dark and evil story. "The Sieur de la Salle was greatly worried when his nephew and servants did not return. He became so uneasy over their long delay that he resolved to go himself to find them. I went with him.

"When we came within sight of the place they were lodged, we saw vultures fluttering near the spot and Sieur de la Salle fired a shot. It was the signal of his death. L'Archeveque appeared and called out to the Commandant to distract his attention while Duhaut hid in the tall weeds. He shot the Sieur de la Salle through the head and he dropped dead on the spot. I ran to his side, but he never spoke a word.

"The rest is too dreadful to think about, but it must be told. Pushing me away and knocking me to the earth, Liotot and Duhaut rushed on the body like furies, stripped it, dragged it naked through the bushes and left it exposed to the ravenous beasts."

There was a long and terrible moment of horrified silence and then Couture was on his feet, crying out to the Abbé Cavelier, "But *you* recovered your brother's body, Father? *You* gave him Christian burial?"

The Abbé's pale face had a tortured look, his voice trembled. "I begged them to let me go to the place and bury my brother and nephew but they refused—"

"Those murderers themselves had a better fate," broke in Joutel bitterly. "The pirate Heins had no part in the slaying of Commandant de la Salle and shortly avenged his death by shooting Duhaut. Liotot was shot down by the pirate's companion, a half-savage Frenchman called Ruter. Duhaut died at once but Liotot lived long enough to make his confession. We dug a grave and buried them together, doing them more honor than they had done our Commandant and his nephew. Although we had no part in their slaying, they met with what they deserved, dying the same death to which they had put others."

"This will be a terrible blow to Captain de Tonti," said Gabriel sadly. "How shall we break the news—"

"We are not going to tell De Tonti my brother is dead," broke in the Abbé quickly.

"What!" exclaimed Couture sharply. "Why should you practice such cruel deceit on a friend so loyal?"

"We must," the Abbé told him earnestly. "Believe me, it would be disastrous if the news of my brother's death became known in Canada before we are able to reach France. I shall simply tell Captain de Tonti that we are under orders to give an account at Court of the discoveries made by my brother and to procure badly needed aid for the suffering colonists."

De Tonti's men stormed in protest. Couture spoke for the others. "What will you tell the captain when he asks for Commandant de la Salle?"

The Abbé's pale blue eyes did not falter before those three indignant faces. He answered like a man who had convinced himself at least that this was the right thing to do. "I shall tell him that my brother brought us part of the way and that he was in good health when I last saw him. That much is true. I was not present at his death."

Gabriel turned an accusing gaze at the young friar. "But you, Father, what will you say if Captain de Tonti asks?"

The Abbé raised a frail hand. "Father Anastasius has promised me to avoid answering any questions. And I expect you," he went on turning to Couture, "to give me your word of honor that you and your men will keep secret all you have heard."

Couture was silent, unable to make up his mind. The Abbé gave him a pleading look. "Promise, my son."

"Well, Father, we shall do as you ask, although I cannot honestly believe that this is fair to the truest friend our Commandant ever had. I'll make one condition: after you are safely out of Canada we'll go ourselves and tell the truth to Captain de Tonti."

"I think you have made a wise decision," said the Abbé, looking at each of them in turn. But somehow, despite his words, the expressions on the faces before him were still very dubious.

Henri de Tonti did not learn the truth about his lost leader until the following spring. When, on April 7, 1688, his little band from the Arkansas brought him the horrible news, he found it hard to accept. The man he loved like a brother, whom he had revered and served with the utmost devotion, had been treacherously murdered more than a year before. And all this time he had not even suspected it!

Impossible to realize that they would never meet again. Unbearable to think that their parting more than four years before when La Salle had left for France had been a last farewell. This was the worst blow he had suffered since that time in far-off Sicily when as a young marine he had wakened in a hospital to find he had no right hand.

But he was never one to brood over sorrows and wrongs. Nothing could change what was done; nothing could be gained by lingering in the unhappy past. So, after his first bitter grief was over, he began to think of what should be done.

Talking the matter over with Gabriel, Couture and De Launay one night not long after the faithful trio had arrived at the fort on the Illinois, he said very earnestly: "I've been thinking about Father Zenobius and the colonists from France stranded on the Gulf of Mexico. It's a long time since the Commandant left them—well over a year—and they're still completely in the dark about the terrible misfortune that befell him."

He began pacing thoughtfully up and down, his dark head bent forward, the black-gloved hand dangling by his side. "How great must be their anxiety and distress without one word from their leader! Someone should go to tell them what has happened. And besides they are in a position of extreme danger—bordering on our ancient foes, the Spaniards, threatened by savages, their ranks depleted by death and disease, their supplies and ammunition lost—"

He stood before them, head raised, eyes glowing with determination. "I'm going to bring them back to my settlement on the Arkansas. They'll be safe there until we can go to the mouth of the Mississippi and finish the work our Commandant began."

"Oh, let's start at once, Captain!" cried Gabriel impetuously. "I long to see Father Zenobius again."

De Tonti was smiling a little. "Ah, Gabriel, I knew I could count on you. Now this is what I want you to do—"

Under the plan he had worked out, Couture and De Launay were to return to Arkansas to guard De Tonti's interests as soon as they were rested and ready to face the long voyage back down the Mississippi. Gabriel would remain and help the captain with the task of manning and equipping his new expedition. De Tonti knew that he would be able to fit out only a small party since he would have to bear all the

expenses now as he had done before when he went down the Mississippi in search of Commandant la Salle. It would cost more money than he had just now, for he was very short of funds.

On his way back to Montreal to embark for France, the Abbé Cavelier had borrowed seven hundred francs from De Tonti. Not a great deal, but it was all the captain could provide. He had given it gladly, not knowing the news the Abbé was hiding from him, and because he thought that such would have been the wish of his leader.

Now he knew his chance of ever receiving repayment of this sum was very slight.

He realized he must raise the funds for his enterprise in the way that lay closest at hand—fur trading. As commandant of Fort St. Louis he enjoyed concessions for dealing in furs with

De Tonti's boat was piled high with cargo.

the Illinois and their allies. Indeed this had been his only source of revenue since La Salle had placed him in charge of the fort when he went back to France in 1683.

During the summer months the furs were not in prime condition and so he had to await that autumn's hunting. As soon as the weather became cold and clear the Indians around the forest sallied forth and killed hundreds of elk, deer and bear. They stalked the buffalo herds, followed the beaver streams. Soon trade at the fort was brisk: tobacco, axes, guns, beads, combs, bracelets were exchanged for the silky brown skins of beaver, thick buffalo hides, bearskins and many other pelts of all sizes.

Captain de Tonti's baggage boat was piled high with valuable cargo when he and Gabriel set out one October morning with three Indians—a Shawnee who had attached himself to the captain and two Iroquois slaves. Their destination was Michilimackinac, the pioneer outpost on the northwest extremity of Lake Huron. Here at the main trading mart for the region the captain sold his furs, bought a large boat and engaged four men for his voyage down the Mississippi.

Two were hardy Canadian voyageurs, Jourdain and Romaine by name. The others, Moreau and Bourdon, were a pair of young sailors, fresh from the waterfronts of France. He would have preferred taking some of his own men from the fort but they could not be spared.

The party of nine reached De Tonti's post on the Arkansas on January 16, 1689. As usual on seeing Chief Iron Hand and his aide Gabriel La Grue, the Quapaws went wild with joy. Nothing would do Chief Sun and Pearl Moon but to hold a huge celebration in their honor. So for a day there were feasting and dancing and the voyageurs would gladly have lingered had it been possible.

It was pleasant, however, to have this brief rest, to be greeted like old friends by the natives, and best of all for the captain to see his men at the settlement and the house that had been built there.

Everything had been provided and was in readiness for his coming, even down to such details as candles made from buffalo tallow. "There are tons of it available," Couture told the captain, "enough to compete with the Irish trade on the European market, once we get our seaport on the Gulf and our river navigation under way."

Ah yes, it was a fine thing to have his own place on the Arkansas, when night came to sit like this before the blazing logs that filled the room with fragrance, the candlelight falling on the papers and maps spread out on the long pine table. De Tonti pored over the descriptions Joutel had left with

Couture of his journeyings with the Abbé and his company. They could be invaluable to the captain in his search.

Only now did he realize the difficulty of this undertaking. The refugees had passed through twenty Indian nations, crossed many rivers, waded through endless swamps. They had followed the trails of the red men and the tracks of the buffalo over hundreds of miles of plains and forests. Surely it was nothing less than a miracle that they had lived to tell it.

De Tonti had taken long hard voyages, but this overland trek through the uncharted southwest was breaking new ground. And he had only a handful of men. He could depend on Gabriel in any emergency, but what of the four newcomers? Would they withstand the hardships?

Nevertheless he kept these thoughts to himself. Outwardly he was confident and optimistic as he mapped out the course they would follow. "We'll float down the Mississippi as far as the country of the Taensas. They've been friendly to us in the past and they'll give us guides and an interpreter when we strike out across country to the west.

"When we reach the village of the Cadodachos we should be on the direct route by which Joutel, the Abbé and their companions struggled out of the wilderness. We'll push on until we come to the country of the Cenis, and there I hope to find the pirate Heins and those who are with him."

Couture nodded. "Joutel told us about them. Two of Heins' men were deserters from La Salle's second journey out of Matagorda in search of the Mississippi—Ruter and Grollet, a pair of half savages."

Gabriel shook his head. "A couple of rascals in Joutel's book, although they were shocked and concerned, so he said, when he told them of the murder of our Commandant and his nephew."

"That's the reason I'm counting on them to guide us the rest of the way to the coast," said De Tonti. "And the old buccaneer Heins himself can't be all bad. At least he avenged our Commandant's death."

For a time after the others had turned in for the night, De Tonti stayed at the table, studying the maps and reading over Joutel's journal in the glow of the flames. After a while, he put them down. In the morning he would find them packed up neatly for the journey.

His face softened as he glanced over at the bunk where Lieutenant La Grue's tall, stalwart frame was outlined. He was lost in sleep, the look of a child on his honest face. What an odd little chap he had been when they'd met so long ago, with his shaved head and savage air! Gabriel was his right hand now. It was a comforting thought.

Exhaustion closed De Tonti's eyes at last and he fell into a restless sleep. He dreamed of Father Zenobius and saw him not in his rough habit but vested for the altar in shining white. He was holding a chalice in both hands, the same silver chalice that he had carried down the Mississippi. And on the friar's good, kind face there was the smile of an angel.

Chapter 9

THE COUNTRY OF THE CENIS

Under De Tonti's leadership the journey proceeded steadily west and then southwest according to plan. There were no serious mishaps although the overland marches through the tangled wilds called for great physical endurance.

The two young sailors from France found it none too easy. But they were highly pleased when they stopped at the villages of friendly Indians they met along the route. The natives were always glad to see the Frenchmen, and the young men feasted and danced and drank the strong beer the red men brewed, for they were a wild reckless pair. De Tonti as usual maintained military discipline but he found these two were hard to manage.

For their part the Canadian boatmen, Jourdain and Romaine, started grumbling as soon as they left the Red

River and hit the trail taken by Joutel's party. "We didn't bargain for anything like this," they complained. "We were hired to navigate the Mississippi."

The feet of the white men bothered them to the point of torment, for their boots wore through and had to be discarded. They wore whatever footgear they could contrive: a piece of green buffalo hide or buckskin fashioned into rude moccasins. Often they had to wade in water up to their knees and when the untanned leather dried on their hot swollen feet, every step was an agony. So when the chance came De Tonti traded with the Indians for fine dressed doeskin to make comfortable shoes. Getting out the trading goods Gabriel gave the Indians four precious steel needles for each skin. The relief when they slipped their weary burning feet into moccasins made from the soft pliant doeskins was bliss itself.

Regardless of such discomforts as these they marched all day long from dawn till after sundown. They ate when they were hungry, a few bites of dried buffalo meat, and when they were thirsty they drank from the nearest stream. At night they made camp on a high river bank that provided safety.

De Tonti drew them on relentlessly; he had a will as iron as his hand. His thoughts were all on the abandoned garrison, the women and children, the little mission among the Indians. Father Anastasius had told him about the work Father Zenobius was doing among the Cenis.

At the village of the Cadodachos, De Tonti had his first news of Heins and his party. Yes, the Indians answered De Tonti's eager questioning, there were white men living over two hundred miles to the west among the Cenis. They were mighty men with lightning sticks that had won them great renown and honor. They had gone off to war with the Cenis and slain many of their enemies.

The Cenis, he was told, were proud to have such men dwelling with them. The white men had helped them win a great victory over their ancient foes to the west and their allies the Spaniards. The Cenis had adopted the white men into their nation; they had married the daughters of chiefs and become like the Cenis themselves.

De Tonti was elated. "Our troubles will be finished when we join them," he told his men. "They'll guide us to the seacoast. Only a few more days and we'll be with them."

"A few more days, Captain?" spoke up Jourdain, one of the Canadians. "Two hundred miles in a few days? By the powers, that's a long way and we're worn out now."

"We'll rest here with this friendly tribe before going on," De Tonti promised. "They'll be glad to have us and we'll get fresh guides from them to show us the best and shortest way."

As it turned out, the Cadodachos really did want them to stay as long as they liked. Chief Palaquechaune was very friendly and led De Tonti to the best lodgings his village could provide. This was the guest house, he explained, where the other white men had stayed. Of course, that must have been the Abbé Cavelier's party. Sergeant Joutel had said that the Cadodachos had urged them not to continue their dangerous journey, but to make their home with them.

Palaquechaune now begged De Tonti to make his home among his people. He addressed him as Chief Iron Hand, for already the Shawnee guide and the Iroquois slaves had spread abroad the greatness of their leader.

"I know you are a mighty chieftain in your own country," he declared. "Stay with us, teach us to use the fire-sticks so we can conquer our enemies. We will give you land, wives, anything you desire. And your companions will be treated in like manner."

De Tonti declined all this and told him they had urgent need to push on to the Cenis. At once the disappointed chief began to raise grave objections. The dangers, he said, were immense, not only from the impassable trails and the many woods and rivers, but worst of all from the Cenis themselves. Strong and powerful they were, to be sure, but fierce as wolves, treacherous as serpents. Using the graphic sign language, Palaquechaune went on to picture the fiendish cruelty of the Cenis. Gestures, rolling eyes, grimaces were charged with horrible meaning.

The Cenis, it seemed, took keen delight in torturing their prisoners and anyone else who aroused the fury of their vengeance. They cut off the ears and noses of their enemies, gouged out their eyes, prolonged their death agonies. Then they cut up their bodies and divided them among the Cenis families who cooked and ate them.

"Cannibals," De Tonti said gravely. "The first we've heard of in these regions." But neither he nor Gabriel were too impressed, having fought the man-eating Iroquois and taken extreme risks. Besides, they realized the chief was exaggerating the danger to suit his own purpose. So De Tonti was not to be moved and only asked one kindness of Palaquechaune: that he would give them guides to conduct them to the Cenis.

Later, as the captain and his aide sat in their tent discussing preparations for the journey, their four white companions stalked in and announced that they were not going on. Determined and badly scared, they carried their arms. And De Tonti knew that a frightened man could be more dangerous and cause more trouble than a brave one.

Jourdain was their spokesman. "Captain, we've talked things over and taken a vote. We all wish to stay here among the Cadodachos. What their chief says makes sense, Captain, good sense."

"Yes," shouted Romaine, the other Canadian, "and it's inhuman to expect us to go—more than flesh and blood can stand."

Moreau, the young sailor, cried out with a shudder: "Who wants to be slaughtered?"

"We're four against two, Captain," said his companion, Bourdon, with desperate bravado. "Don't try to push us too far."

De Tonti heard them out in silence. They had turned out worse than he had feared, and he realized he had no command over them. Given the chance, they were quite capable of shooting him in the back. This was mutiny, but he must accept it and try to make the best of it. If the revolt spread to the Shawnee and the two Iroquois slaves, he would indeed be in trouble.

"Very well, men," he told them quietly. "You leave me no course but to agree. I ask only this of you—don't let our Indians know you have abandoned me. Let them think I am sending you back to the Quapaws with the news that we have located the men who were with La Salle and are going on with them to the seacoast. At least, the savages will not suspect our disunion."

Somewhat shamefaced at their sorry behavior, the rebels consented to keep their desertion secret. What was asked of them was but a small favor. This unflinching De Tonti of the iron hand had driven them harder than anyone they had ever served under, but neither had he spared himself. And he'd been fair and just in his dealings.

Chief Palaquechaune gave De Tonti five Cadodachos as guides, and it was a relief in a way to be free of the sulky white men with their mutterings and complaints. The captain still had Gabriel La Grue who was worth more than the four of them put together. The Shawnee and the two slaves completed the party that struck out for the Cenis country.

It was early April when they left, and the month was almost over when they caught their first sight of the round thatched roofs of the Cenis. They were nearing the largest village they had seen in their travels, an odd-looking settlement with wide conical-shaped dwellings, each built to house several families.

They came to a tall spreading tree and saw carved on its great trunk a cross and the arms of France. Well they knew who had placed them there! De Tonti and Gabriel stood at salute, remembering the other times—days of valor and adventure, good times and bad, carefree and anxious—all clouded now by the tragic finish to a life of high achievement.

De Tonti sighed. "The Sieur de la Salle had more courage and less luck than any man I ever knew. A man of wonderful ability, Gabriel, capable of undertaking any venture."

They found the village quiet and deserted except for the women and children and a few old men squatting in the sun. De Tonti questioned them and learned that the pirate Heins and his crew had gone off with the Cenis chiefs and warriors to fight the Spaniards. No one could say when they would return; no one thought it would be soon.

This meant the collapse of the hopeful plans De Tonti had built around meeting Heins and his companions. But it did not shake his determination to rescue the survivors at Matagorda Bay. "We can surely find a few Cenis guides to show us the way," he decided. "Make them understand what we want, Gabriel, and offer them our most tempting inducements."

Gabriel was an expert at the sign language and could tell that the Indians understood him. But they shook their heads and granted in the negative. For some puzzling reason no one wanted to go to the seacoast, not for the highly prized hatchets and knives, not for the biggest, shiniest rings and necklaces in De Tonti's dazzling collection of cut glass.

Never before had they met with such baffling apathy. Or was it just indifference? De Tonti thought he saw a mocking light in the eyes of more than one, as if they were laughing at some secret joke. He had a sudden feeling that they were hiding their real reason for not guiding him to the coast.

"Take me to the one the chief has left to act in his place," he said finally.

The Indians led him to the house of Three Horns, the high priest, who lived beside their temple. He was a squat dark man with small crafty eyes like two jet beads and a big ugly mouth. But De Tonti scarcely noticed his features so horrified was he to see that over his naked misshapen body Three Horns wore a long filthy mantle of silk that had once been white. It was open at the front and fastened at the breast with a tarnished metal clasp. He had seen many like it, for this was a cope such as is worn by a Catholic priest at Benediction.

Then he saw something more—something that turned him even colder with horror. On a rude shelf against the wall stood Father Zenobius' small silver chalice.

He looked at Gabriel, saw the color drain from his face and read his own shocked discovery in his aide's startled eyes. Now he understood, now all was painfully clear to him.

The Cenis refused to take them to the garrison on the coast because no one was there. These Indians had killed them all—slain Father Zenobius and the other colonists!

With flashing eyes De Tonti turned and accused the Cenis of this frightful crime. Three Horns said nothing and stared at him banefully, but some of the village women who had gathered around began to cry. And De Tonti knew that he had not been wrong.

Later all was confirmed by one of De Tonti's Indians. From an old man among the Cenis he learned more of the dreadful massacre that had ended La Salle's ill-starred attempt to found a colony at the mouth of the Mississippi. The Cenis had attacked the unprotected garrison almost two years before—in 1687—the same year La Salle had left it on his last fatal journey.

De Tonti needed to go no farther. He exchanged hatchets and glass beads for some horses the Cenis had stolen from the Spaniards. Mounted upon them, he and his companions turned back toward the Mississippi.

Chapter 10
The Arkan$as Post

"I never suffered so much in my life as on this journey."
Henri de Tonti, the man of iron, made this admission as he half-reclined on a buffalo robe before his log house on the Arkansas. It was a bright hot August day and the breeze from the river, the cool shade of the trees were grateful after the burning siege of swamp fever from which he was recovering.

Couture and De Launay were asking the captain and Gabriel about their travels back from the Cenis country, trying to draw from them the whole painful story. And now that he'd learned French, Sun Eagle was an eager listener too.

The captain reclined before his log house.

Gabriel was finding it hard to tell of all they'd been through in any language; somehow mere words didn't seem adequate. "I can never describe the trouble we had getting out of that miserable country where it rained day and night. The floods and the swamps and nothing to eat —well, I don't see how we survived."

"We didn't know what real hardship was until we left the Cadodachos," said De Tonti taking up the story. "We reached their village on May 10 and stayed a week to rest our horses. They gave us a guide but he didn't last long."

"The captain's horse drowned," Gabriel explained, "and the guide was so afraid of being punished that he ran away to his people. That left our party to find its way alone. After that our troubles began in real earnest."

De Tonti nodded. "The spring rains had begun and the streams were rising. I directed our course to the southeast and we marched over a hundred and twenty miles. It was rough going, no sun to travel by, no moon to light the night. We crossed seven streams, all of them swollen. When we got to the Coroas River we had to stop. The whole country was drowned in the overflow.

"Finding no dry land anywhere, we made a raft to cross to the other side of the river. We came to the conclusion that we'd have to abandon our horses. That was a hard decision to make, believe me. But it was impossible to take them through floods like that."

"Didn't you meet any Indians?" Couture asked.

"We did, once just as we'd left the horses and were getting ready to embark on our raft. We called and called to them but they were frightened and ran away. I hope they came back after we left and rescued the poor faithful creatures."

"You must have missed the horses sorely," said De Launay.

"Oh, we did," exclaimed Gabriel. "Sometimes we had to drag our baggage over large tracts of reed-covered prairie. They seemed endless. We crossed miles and miles of flooded country."

"And in all that desolate expanse," resumed De Tonti, "we found just one little island of dry land. Our provisions were running low but we did have the good fortune to kill a bear. We ate what we needed and dried the rest of the meat to take with us.

"We had to sleep on the trunks of trees that we lashed together. We made our fires on the trees and that wasn't easy, for the rains came down with no letup—sometimes in solid sheets like a wall. We were marooned, cut off from the rest of the world. No shelter anywhere. I had a horrible feeling that we were the last survivors on earth—"

His voice trailed off and he lay back, looking up at the sky. Today there wasn't a single cloud in the deep blue vault. The murmur of the river lapping against the shore was soothing. His eyes closed.

"The captain was smitten with fever," said Gabriel, dropping his voice. "At times he shook all over and I could hear his teeth rattling. Then he would burn like fire, even though he was soaked with rain—we all were—and he could never seem to satisfy his thirst. It was terrible.

"Then our food gave out. There were no animals to be found in the flooded waste. We had nothing left, nothing but water—oceans and oceans of it. We went three days without a bite to eat. We couldn't have lasted much longer, but God was good to us. On the evening of the third day we reached the village of the Coroas.

"I couldn't begin to tell you the joy we felt. It was July 14, almost two months since we had started homeward. It seemed more like two years. The Coroas feasted us for as many days as we'd starved, but the captain couldn't eat. The food sent his fever raging. To tell the truth, there were times when I never thought I'd get him here alive—"

Off in the distance two shots sounded deep in the forest. "That must be Jourdain and Romaine," Couture remarked. "Sounds as if we're going to have another brace of turkeys for supper."

A smile chased the gloom from Gabriel's face. "Ever since we picked those two up at the Coroas village they've been trying to make amends for their desertion. It was generous of Captain de Tonti to take them back."

The shots had roused De Tonti in time to hear the last remark. He sat up, yawning and feeling rested and very comfortable. "Oh, there are times when one must make allowances, you know. Poor wretches, they soon found what life among the Indians was like and were trying to make their way back here somehow. When they saw us they were so glad and so contrite it was pathetic."

Sun Eagle had been silently taking in everything. "Chief Iron Hand," he said gravely, "the red men did not desert you."

"They were faithful all the way," cried De Tonti warmly, "and I'll never forget it. When I get back to Fort St. Louis I'm going to free the two Iroquois. They deserve it."

Gabriel approved heartily. "Yes, sir, they've really earned their freedom. Without them I don't see how we could have survived."

Sun Eagle was happy for the Iroquois. "I know what it's like to be a prisoner of war," he recalled, his dark eyes somber. "It's a long time ago but I can still remember."

For a little while they were silent, thinking of the strange way they had met years ago across the great river in the land of the Chickasaws. And they thought of one who would come no more to them, the good kind friend in the gray robe.

Coming swiftly toward them from the house, Star Mary interrupted their musings. She wore a short white doeskin tunic with shoulder straps of many-colored beads and at the hem a broad border of the same gay bangles, Smiling she held out a small pottery mug. 'Time for your medicine, Chief Iron Hand," she said, speaking the French words in a soft slur that was quite charming.

De Tonti made a laughing grimace as he downed the bitter dose. "My fever's all gone. How much longer must you doctor me?"

"This is the last. It's a tonic to bring back the appetite."

"Ah, you have a wonderful notion of healing potions, my dear, and you're a born nurse. I'll never forget the way you and Gabriel have taken care of me."

Gabriel was on his feet, smiling down at Star Mary with admiration and something deeper in his candid gaze. Star Mary's beautiful hazel eyes were all aglow too as she looked at him. Friends who had known and liked each other for a long time, these two had been drawn very close during the weeks they had watched so faithfully together at De Tonti's bedside.

Together they strolled down to the river bank where Sun Eagle was getting ready to start the canoe back to the village. De Tonti's gaze was understanding as it rested on the Canadian youth motionless on the bank, watching the canoe take Star Mary away.

The towering heights of the forest trees blotted out the sunlight, the rippling waves were dappled with their giant shadows. It was so quiet, so lonely, Gabriel could hear Star Mary's voice coming back to him over the waters. She was singing a Quapaw love song, a sad little refrain about a pair of true lovers who had to part.

The radiant, happy look had gone from the young man's face when he turned back from the river. He seemed to have something on his mind—something that was making him miserable. As he flung himself down near De Tonti, the others rose and began moving toward the house.

The captain laid his hand on his young aide's arm. "My boy, you could never find a lovelier girl—"

"Oh, I know that, sir," Gabriel spoke out quickly. "But you're better now and we must leave for the north—"

"No, Gabriel," De Tonti corrected with a smile. "I must leave. But I want you to stay here at the post, for it's plain to see your heart is here."

Gabriel's face, open as a book, was a study in mixed emotions. "But if I stay with the Quapaws that means you and I will be separated. I never wanted that to happen."

"I know, but you're a man now and must live your own life. It will be a good life here among the Beautiful People and I need you here to guard my interests. Do not look so sad; we will meet again and share other adventures, I promise you."

And so it was that Gabriel La Grue remained at the Arkansas settlement and married Star Mary.

Chapter 11

WHAT HAPPENED AFTERWARD

Captain de Tonti, leaving the Arkansas post in charge of his aides, returned to Fort St. Louis where he wasted no time in pursuing his flourishing fur trade. If his failure to rescue the colonists and to carry out La Salle's plans gnawed at him, he kept it to himself. Henri de Tonti was not a man to brood about the past.

He never lost interest in his settlement on the Arkansas, although he was never able to remain there for any length of time. He sent more men to develop the pioneer colony, he saw that a garrison and warehouse were built, a trading post established. In 1699 he brought the first priest to reside there—Father Nicolas Foucault—who labored there with great success and led many of the Quapaws to become Christians.

Then after ten years a strange thing happened. The time-worn letter that Captain de Tonti had left for La Salle with the Quinipassas years before fell into the hands of another explorer, Canadian-born naval hero Pierre le Moyne, Sieur de Iberville. The same enthusiasm that had kindled La Salle's

Iberville asked De Tonti to start on another expedition.

imagination now took hold of Iberville. He sent for De Tonti and asked him to help him organize another expedition to navigate the Mississippi and establish a colony on the Gulf coast. He knew that he had the right man in De Tonti. No other man of his time had gone up and down the river more often than the captain. No one else knew its bends and currents so well as he; no one else could treat as successfully with the Indians along its shores.

De Tonti fell in with the plan at once. It meant the fulfillment of La Salle's plans for colonization—a fulfillment that meant as much to the captain as it had to his leader. The intrepid fur trader immediately began recruiting a party and soon had fifty expert voyageurs, including Gabriel La Grue and Sun Eagle. In 1702, manning ten canoes, they paddled down the Mississippi to join Iberville's party.

Iberville and his brother Bienville had already explored the mouth of the Mississippi and the Gulf coast east as far as Florida. They were ready now to found a permanent settlement. The place they had chosen was a choice site at the mouth of the Mobile River in the land of the Alibamon nation.

There they built Fort Mobile, the first fortified French settlement and garrison on the Gulf. Captain de Tonti became its commandant while Gabriel La Grue and Sun Eagle returned to the Arkansas country. Soon the captain held the same high position on the Gulf as he had for over twenty years on the Illinois River. Here too he gained the respect and admiration of the Indian nations, held them in firm alliance to France and led them to war against their enemies.

For two years De Tonti governed Fort Mobile and defended the little colony with daring and courage. Then the scourge of the Gulf coast struck. An epidemic of yellow fever swept Fort Mobile leaving death and fear behind it. Henri de Tonti was one of the first to fall ill.

As he lay racked with fever he thought of his comrades in adventure: of La Salle, afraid of nothing, the most heroic man he had ever known; of Gabriel La Grue, his young aide who had been so faithful and idealistic; of Father Zenobius, gentle and zealous for souls. He was a lucky man, he thought, to have spent so much of his life among friends like these. All the hardship and danger had been worth the effort. Henri de Tonti closed his eyes.

He did not open them again. On September 6, 1704, the yellow fever claimed another victim. De Tonti of the Iron Hand who had survived so much was dead. Back at the Arkansas post Gabriel and Star Mary mourned him as if he had been their true father. Through them and through the other men that he had trained, his work at the posts and settlements was continued and on their sites grew some of the greatest cities of the American interior.

History has not accorded De Tonti the fame and glory given the explorers whose battle he fought. He always willingly took the second place and perhaps that was the reason. But when the long story of his intrepid deeds is weighed and compared with others, the faithful aide steps up to take his rightful niche in the history of the Mississippi Valley. For this man with the iron hand was as great, if not greater, than the leaders he followed.

Author's Note

Perhaps nowhere else have the name and the fame of Henri de Tonti been cherished and perpetuated as in Arkansas where he founded the first white settlement west of the Mississippi River and the future territorial capital, Arkansas Post. The works of local historians and Indian relics preserved in the Arkansas History Commission museum at Little Rock greatly simplified the research required for this phase of De Tonti's explorations. Especially helpful were such books as Halliburton's *History of Arkansas County*, Herndon's *History of Arkansas*, and Allsop's *Romantic Arkansas*.

Space does not permit reference to the factual evidence found in the old landmarks and records in and around Arkansas County where the Post is located. The township in which the county seat is situated, for example, is named La Grue, as is a large bayou of that section.

However, the main theme of my story required research of a much broader scope, for which I am largely indebted to Congressman W. F. Norrell of Arkansas who made available to me from the Congressional Library rare translations containing the original journals and memoirs written by De Tonti, Father Membré, and Henri Joutel. Without such invaluable sources, this book could never have been written. I would also like to acknowledge my gratitude to Senator John L. McClellan of Arkansas and Senator John F. Kennedy of Massachusetts for their willingness to aid.

Helpful also were Chesnel's *History of Cavelier de La Salle,* DuPratz' *History of Louisiana,* and Murphy's *Henry de Tonty, Fur Trader of the Mississippi,* copies of which were provided by the Garland County Library, Hot Springs, Arkansas. I wish to express my thanks to Mrs. E. H. Belk, the librarian, and her staff for their kind interest.

CPSIA information can be obtained
at www.ICGtesting.com
Printed in the USA
LVHW08s2326160918
590346LV00025B/453/P